BOLT ACTION — WEIRD WORLD WAR II WARGAMES RULES

KONFLIKT '47
RESURGENCE

Osprey Games, an imprint of Osprey Publishing Ltd
c/o Bloomsbury Publishing Plc
PO Box 883, Oxford, OX1 9PL, UK
Or
c/o Bloomsbury Publishing Inc.
1385 Broadway, 5th Floor, New York, NY 10018
E-mail: info@ospreypublishing.com

www.ospreygames.co.uk

OSPREY and OSPREY GAMES are trademarks of Osprey Publishing Ltd, a division
of Bloomsbury **Publishing Plc.**

First published in Great Britain in 2017

A CIP catalogue record for this book is available from the British Library.

ISBN: PB: 9781472826503
        ePub: 9781472826510
        ePDF: 9781472826497
        XML: 9781472826527

17 18 19 20 21   10 9 8 7 6 5 4 3 2 1

Typeset in Univers and ITC Machine
Originated by PDQ Digital Media Solutions, Bungay, UK
Printed in Hong Kong through Worldprint Ltd.

Osprey Publishing supports the Woodland Trust, the UK's leading woodland
conservation charity. Between 2014 and 2018 our donations are being spent on
their Centenary Woods project in the UK.

***

Warlord Games Ltd.
The Howitt Wing, Lenton Business Centre, Lenton Boulevard,
Nottingham, NG7 2BY, UK
E-mail: info@warlordgames.com

For more information on Bolt Action Konflikt '47 and other products, please visit
www.warlordgames.com

Clockwork Goblin
54 Bibury Road, Cheltenham, GL51 6AY, UK
E-mail: clockworkgoblinminis@gmail.com

CONTENTS

NEW SCENARIOS AND RULES   84

CREDITS   100

INTRODUCTION

This book is the first supplement for *Konflikt '47* and aims to develop the original rulebook in a number of different directions. The largest addition is the much anticipated Imperial Japanese Army Lists, but Finnish players will find out what has befallen their country in the latter years of the war as well. We have also taken this opportunity to consolidate the errata and clarifications that have cropped up since the release of the core rulebook. Players of the original four armies in the rulebook will also find something new as we develop the specialist units and characters of their nations.

The book is divided into five sections. The first details further background to the *Konflikt '47* universe. The second covers the new rules and errata, as well as the rules for playing vehicle- or walker-heavy platoons in *Konflikt '47*. Then we add new units to the existing nations. Next up, we introduce the complete Japanese and Finnish Army Lists. Finally, we provide some new scenarios and their associated special rules for players to enjoy, with a specific *Konflikt '47* flavour to their narrative.

*Imperial Japanese
Army Exoskeleton Trooper*

BACKGROUND AND HISTORY

This supplement adds some more information regarding the history and backstory of the *Konflikt '47* universe. Chronologically, the northern flank is introduced, depicting the fate of Finland as it is caught between the German and Russian juggernauts. Across the world, an additional three months of history is added, bringing the timeline from March 1947 to the beginning of June 1947.

WESTERN EUROPE

NOVEMBER 1946–FEBRUARY 1947

With the Western European theatre gripped in the most severe winter in living memory, the first months of the new year are a period of re-armament and re-organisation for both sides. Germany, with renewed morale after the victories of 1946, uses the time to refit its tired and battered units with the latest vehicles and equipment. Ammunition and a new synthetic fuel arrive at frontline units in unprecedented quantities, and German commanders take the chance to train and drill their newest recruits and conscripts. Likewise, the Allies move vast mountains of resources across from the Normandy beachheads and the heavy ports in Antwerp and Amsterdam. The industrial might of the US is going to be a decisive factor in the fighting to come.

Part of this industry is focussed on the re-armament of the French Army. General de Gaulle's triumphant return to Paris in November 1944 was followed with a rapid call to arms and the French population responded. Although eager to exact their revenge on their former occupiers, the French Army is prepared carefully through 1946, with a focus on training and quality over quantity. Equipped along US lines, the French Army is poised to field four corps of heavily equipped and highly trained forces at the start of 1947. Larger infantry formations provide rear area security across France. The US, having already equipped the First French Army, begins adding Heavy Armoured Infantry and M8 Grizzly walkers to the French order of battle. A similar story is unfolding in Italy, where the Royalist Italian Forces of southern Italy are keen to prove their value to the Allied cause and are equipped from the industrial stockpiles of the US. The Allies remain cautious of the Italian's will to fight their fellow countrymen, and although well equipped with conventional vehicles and weapons, Italian access to Rift-tech weaponry is limited.

Despite this impressive display of industrial muscle, at night, German Rift-tech monstrosities continue to raid Allied lines, ensuring units never truly get a chance to fully relax on the front lines. To counter this, the enhanced soldiers of the US Paragon Programme often set traps for the Shreckwulfen and Nachtjäger, and achieve a high success rate, but the Paragons can't be everywhere and the average Allied soldier spends the night watchful and fearful.

Although the weather prevents the easy movement of forces, the US pushes its new Rift-tech formations to forward staging posts in anticipation of a spring offensive. Brigade formations of Heavy Armoured Infantry, supported by Pershing and Tesla-armed tanks, prepare to throw the Germans back across the Rhine. However, their preparations are matched by Germany; Shock Brigades of fanatical SS troops are being made ready to storm out of the beachheads to try and repeat the blitzkrieg tactics of seven years earlier.

Heavy metal! German panzers and walkers combine with infantry support

MARCH 1947

As the worst of the weather begins to break, the lull in fighting rapidly comes to an end. Looking to seize the initiative, the combined French–US 7th Army, under General Patch, pushes forward at Karlsruhe. The objective is to crush the German beachhead on the west bank of the Rhine and open a gap in the German defences to the south of the main Allied effort further north. Starting on 13 March and acting within the spirit of Eisenhower's intent, but before the British and other American forces were co-ordinated, Patch takes a huge gamble that almost pays off. Striking the prepared German defences hard, the 7th Army succeeds in penetrating deep into the beachhead, but at tremendous cost. German reinforcements slow the US advance and then bring it to a halt.

On 22 March, French forces attempt to rebuild momentum with a thrust north towards Mannheim, but after initial success they stall well short of their objective. Even so, the German defensive line has been penetrated and the Allies have caused enough damage that any German plans to advance in the sector are thwarted. However, 7th Army now has Germans to its front and flanks, and the decision has to be made whether to withdraw or prepare to defend the territory seized. To Patch, the decision is simple: hold and reinforce the breach. His efforts to convince Eisenhower to provide more resources are echoed by de Gaulle, keen to see the French flag at the forefront of the renewed offensive.

Elsewhere, the Allies are more cautious and initial probes in the British and Canadian sectors reveal strong defensive positions with few signs of weakness. Reluctant to commit forces without clear objectives, the activity in the northern sectors of the front are characterised by a series of raids and reconnaissance- in-force operations. On 19 March, the British use their new Meteor rockets for the first time, with 5 Royal Tank Regiment's newly issued Churchills attempting to punch through a German strongpoint as a test of this new Rift-tech weapon. Results are good, but a more concentrated effort is going to be required to create a breakthrough.

In the centre, the US 3rd Army under General Patton conducts similar operations, and likewise finds little evidence of a weakness to exploit. With Patch calling for reinforcements for the 7th Army, General Bradley opts to continue with raids and probes in the north, confident that an opportunity will reveal itself.

On the Gustav Line in Italy, the improving weather gives each side the opportunity to determine the other's intent. It is rapidly clear to the Germans and Italians defending the fortifications across the centre of the country that the Allies are in little better shape to attack than they were before the winter lull. Whilst a boost to the defender's morale, the knowledge is of little military use as the Axis forces are well dug in and prepared, and see no reason to risk defeat by going on the offensive. One battle of note on 9 March, north of the Sangro River, sees two units of Italian troops encounter each other in simultaneous recce operations. Perhaps as neither force wants to seem weak in front of their allies, the meeting engagement leads to significant commitment of additional forces. After a full days fighting, both sides withdraw, having fought fiercely and acquitted themselves well. Allied and Axis concerns over the reliability of their Italian allies are allayed, at least for the time being.

APRIL–MAY 1947

With initial efforts to gain the initiative less effective than desired, Eisenhower orders twin offensive efforts in the north and south. In the north, Montgomery is tasked with forcing a path to the Rhine and into the Ruhr to target Germany's industrial facilities in the region. Under orders, the Canadian 1st Army crosses the start line first and pushes hard for the Rhine. Gradual progress is made but German defences prove costly to assault and dangerous to bypass. By the start of May, the Rhine seems in reach but the majority of the 1st Army's combat power is spent.

With the offensive stalling, Montgomery orders Dempsey's British 2nd Army into the fight to attempt to secure the gains made by the Canadians. However, confusion during the forward passage of lines loses the Allies precious time, allowing German forces the opportunity to launch Operation *Trident*, the offensive they have been preparing for during the winter months. Crossing the Dutch–German border on a narrow front between Roermond and Venlo, the lead elements of Army Group B punch deep in to Dempsey's weakened lines. With 5th Panzer Army leading the German advance, they make rapid progress against thinly spread British forces. Their objective is the Dutch port of Antwerp (with secondary objectives of Brussels and Rotterdam), which is critical to the flow of Allied raw material into Europe. At the end of May, the Germans are fighting for Eindhoven in a combined panzer and Fallschirmjäger assault. Bitter fighting between British and German forces rages from street to street. The pinnacle of German Rift-tech equipment is fielded to maximise every advantage, from heavy-armoured grenadiers and panzermechs to Shreckwulfen and Nachtjäger skirmishers terrorising the night. With forward elements further north and fatigued by their attempted assault, Dempsey's 1st Army is in disarray and the Canadian 1st Army is rapidly thrown into the fight to stall the German advance.

Patch's 7th Army is locked in combat with the German 1st Army in the vicinity of Karlsruhe. Using the Black Forest to the south, the Germans are able to raid and harass the flanks of Patch's forces. As the French 2nd Corps prepares to push northeast in response, it is surprised by a German offensive

Death from Above! the hated Nachtjägers swoop down onto Soviets

directed by Himmler himself. In an attempt to cut off large parts of the 7th Army, Himmler strikes west, seizing Gambsheim and threatening to cut deep into the rear of Patch's forces. This is followed by frantic efforts to stall the German advance by both US and French forces, many of whom are badly mauled as they enter the combat zone in piecemeal fashion.

In Italy, after a series of probes to confirm the solidity of the Gustav Line, Allied commanders face an experienced opponent in Field Marshal Kesselring, and he is not about to surrender his superior position easily. The US 5th Army makes the first attempt to breach the German and Italian defences but have little appetite for the casualties inflicted upon them by well-positioned and well-trained Axis forces. With little direction forthcoming from both high commands, the Allied and Axis forces in Italy are content to dig in and watch each other carefully across no-man's land.

JUNE 1947

This is now…

FINLAND AND THE NORTHERN FLANK

1941–44

At the launch of Germany's Operation *Barbarossa*, Finland is a reluctant ally and participant: with no other nation willing to support its efforts against a belligerent Soviet Union, Germany offered assistance and Finland accepted. Working with Germany in the planning of the northern element of *Barbarossa*, Finnish and German units fight together until December 1941, recapturing territory lost to Russia in the 1939–40 Winter War. With Russia distracted on many other fronts, and Germany unable to create any meaningful pressure on Russia from the far north, the Finnish and German troops dig in to defend their gains and the front remains relatively calm.

Finnish Jääkäri

MARCH 1944

President Roosevelt calls for Finland to distance itself from Germany but provides no reassurances of material or financial support to compensate for this high-risk strategic decision. Finland finds itself standing at odds with the Allies whilst facing an increasingly aggressive Soviet Union, with no sign of any assistance coming from the Western Powers to replace the support it receives from Germany.

APRIL–AUGUST 1944

Recognising Finland's fragile position geographically, and with Germany suffering a series of reverses in Europe, Russia steps up its pressure on Finland to return the territory gained in the 1941 conflict.

SEPTEMBER–OCTOBER 1944

With increased pressure on Germany from the Soviet Union, Finland decides its position is increasingly untenable and enters into an uneasy ceasefire with Russia. Russia's demands are simple: turn against the Germans in Finland. Many in Finland are uncomfortable with this position and through various miscommunications and poor military decisions, the German Army is largely allowed to leave northwards into Norway with minimal losses or resistance. This also allows them to protect the vital nickel mines in the region. Russia is furious at what it sees as a betrayal of trust and deliberate negligence by Finland, and the ceasefire barely holds. Finland engages in sporadic hostilities against German forces in Norway in an effort to appease Russian anger.

NOVEMBER–DECEMBER 1944

Unknown to the Soviet Union, and also to many in Finland, nearly 2,000 Finnish volunteers move into northern Norway with the retreating Germans. These volunteers are formed into the SS Freiwilligen Battalion Nordost and are equipped and resupplied by Germany. Meanwhile, the Finnish Army returns previously captured Soviet armour and heavy weapons. An uneasy ceasefire holds along the Russia–Finland front, but politically the two nations are hard-pressed to reach common understanding on any regional issues.

JANUARY–AUGUST 1945

The front with Russia remains broadly quiet; Russia's attention is firmly focussed to the south maintaining its pressure on the retreating Germans. Within Finland an active underground organisation grows, declaring Russia as a greater threat than Germany and demanding an increase in the nation's defences. The Resistance encourages young patriots to prepare for war with Russia and creates an underground movement of men northwards into Norway for training with the SS Freiwilligen Battalion Nordost. Many choose to stay with the unit and it grows to regimental size, adding an artillery and small armoured battalion.

Soviet Ursus Infantry

IJA Gaikokkaku Exoskeleton

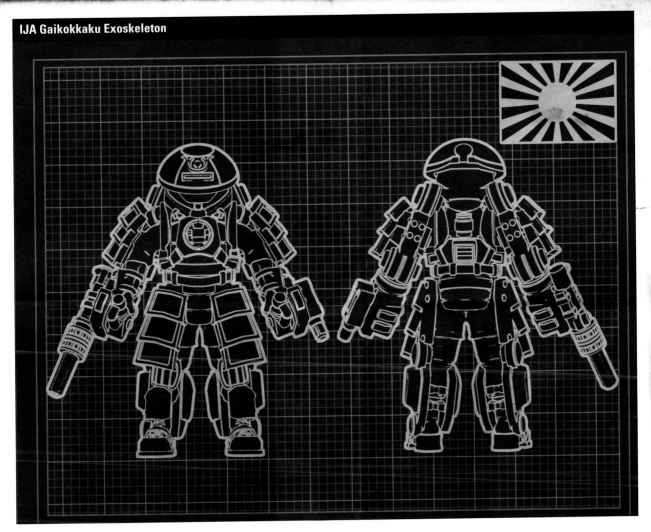

SEPTEMBER–OCTOBER 1945

The Soviet Embassy is attacked by the Resistance on 19 September, causing considerable damage and the death of the Soviet ambassador to Finland. Frantic and earnest efforts to appease the Soviets by the Finnish government are in vain. On 12 September 1945, the Soviet Union launches a full invasion of Finland. Unlike 1940, the Finns are in no position to resist the now-experienced and often battle-hardened Soviet formations, and the country sues for peace by the end of October. The Soviet invasion is not without its difficulties, and numerous instances of bravery and military fortitude leads the fledgling underground movement in to becoming an active Resistance, which the Soviets accuse of being equipped by the US and Germany in equal measure.

NOVEMBER 1945–FEBRUARY 1946

The flow of volunteers into the Resistance increases. The Germans enthusiastically back the Finnish Resistance that proves to be a constant thorn in the side of the Soviet occupiers. Russia is forced to hold far more troops in Finland than it desires, and the relationship with the local population is eroded with each of the harsh reprisals Soviet commanders inflict on unarmed civilians. The Resistance continues to send volunteers north; the SS Freiwilligen Battalion Nordost becomes almost a Finnish army in exile, being renamed the SS Freiwilligen Division Nordost as a result. Public opinion swings firmly against the Soviet occupiers and with no aid forthcoming from any other quarter, Germany is seen as the only effective solution to the Russian problem.

MARCH 1946

The 27th Jäger Battalion is reformed as part of the SS Freiwilligen Division with specific orders to facilitate and enhance Resistance operations in Finland. The impact of these veterans is considerable and Soviet garrison troops, often of mixed quality, find themselves firmly in hostile territory and confined to small areas of safety. This is particularly true in the north, where Soviet convoys and patrols are regularly ambushed and captured.

APRIL–OCTOBER 1946

In a concerted and well-orchestrated operation in April 1946, the Resistance, led by teams of Kaukopartio troops, conduct attacks on three of Finland's major rail hubs. The raids are timed to strike at large concentrations of Soviet supplies and equipment holdings. Although hugely successful, repercussions ordered from Stalin himself see scores of civilians shot in town squares in reprisal. The situation in Finland reaches a new low for the Soviet occupiers, with effectively no assistance from the local population. Their occupation is limited to numerous heavily fortified enclaves in and around the major cities of the country. Fully occupied further south in Europe, and with the morale of Soviet forces already at a very low level, the Russian Army in Finland digs in to await fresh orders and reinforcements.

NOVEMBER 1946–FEBRUARY 1947

The winter to end all winters hits all of Europe and especially the Scandinavian countries. Even the winter-hardened Soviet and Finnish troops struggle to operate in the weather. However, the Finnish Resistance launches Operation *Tursas* in a small break in the weather. On 4 December 1946, a co-ordinated strike on communication towers, generators and fuel dumps plunges the Soviet occupiers into a dangerous situation. Struggling to repair the damage in the weather, smaller outposts are abandoned as a lack of heating and communication shatters morale. The Soviet occupiers are forced to retreat to larger compounds and garrisons to protect themselves from both the Resistance and the weather. Most garrisons in the north either flee south or go silent.

Meanwhile in Norway, the Germans invest heavily in the highly motivated force of Finns, who are keen to exact a price from the Soviet forces occupying their country. The SS Freiwilligen Division Nordost is developed into a combined arms divisional group, and more significantly is entrusted with German Rift-tech developed equipment. Heavy Infantry armour is only provided in small numbers as the Finns find its lack of mobility ill-suited to their tactics, but Spinne panzermechs are issued in significant numbers and a battalion of Jääkäri paratroopers are fitted with the latest Falcon armour. A small cadre of the more fanatical Finnish soldiers volunteer for the Shreckwulfen programme, and even Nachtjägers are reported within the units deemed most loyal to the German cause. Within the Division, a clear divide begins to emerge between those who are clearly pro-German and a larger, patriotically anti-Soviet group, although no apparent discord is evident.

MARCH–MAY 1947

As the winter breaks, or at least becomes more manageable in the north, Soviet relief columns attempt to reach their beleaguered garrisons across Finland. The Finns are, however, one step ahead and are waiting for them. The convoys are repeatedly ambushed and often destroyed, not just by Resistance fighters, but by military formations from the SS Freiwilligen Division Nordost which has crossed the border and is operating from northern Finland. Operation *Ukko* is a concerted attack on all Russian garrisons in the north and pushes south to Ylieveska in the west and Tailvalkosi in the east. However, Soviet weight of numbers begins to stall the operation and the Finns pull back north, drawing the Russians into planned ambushes and even onto prepared German formations lying in wait for them.

JUNE 1947

This is now…

---

12 MARCH 1947: SOMEWHERE NEAR IVALO

A Soviet relief column approaches from the south, heading for the garrison in Ivalo, but encounters Finnish ski troops escorted by Spinne light panzermechs harassing the now burning garrison. Keen to engage the Finnish raiders, the convoy's escort of T-34 tanks move forward but strike mines laid off the main roadways. In the confusion the raiders retire north, heading into dense forests for cover.

Continuing to the garrison, the convoy is ambushed a mere 300m from its destination. Snipers kill exposed tank commanders, whilst a pair of concealed PaK 40 anti-tank guns exact a further toll on the tanks escorting the relief column. As the Soviets turn to fight through the ambushing guns, a heavier retort echoes out from the treeline and the leading T-34 is punched backwards as a heavier anti-tank rounds stops it dead. From the trees emerges a white Zeus, bearing Finnish markings, flanked by the returning Spinnes. The Soviet column is soon reduced to burning wrecks with survivors fleeing on foot, chased down by the Spinnes.

Rumours spread through the Russian Army of this ghostly Zeus, and stories of a new White Death are once again told in hushed tones.

Siberian terror troops assault a German patrol

EASTERN EUROPE

NOVEMBER 1946–FEBRUARY 1947

The most savage winter in memory proves too much for the German Army and its momentum is forced to a halt. Even the resilient Soviets are hard pressed to operate in conditions that mirror the worst their country can offer. The Soviets are, however, able to consolidate after their setbacks in the north. Life for the cut off Soviet forces in Danzig borders on the unbearable, with a lack of fuel and food, and the garrison fights a constant battle for survival. Heroic efforts by the Soviet Navy, supported by the Soviet Air Force, manage to deliver the bare minimum of supplies to the encircled forces.

In the Balkans, the various guerrilla and partisan bands are forced into inactivity as many perish to the elements in the countryside. German and Soviet special forces, often supported by Rift-tech super-soldiers, ensure the war is not forgotten, but the tempo falls to its lowest ebb.

The Red Army spends a lot of time moving newer and more modern equipment forward. The anti-tank walker variant of the Mammoth, the Mastodon, is completed and put into operational service. Owing much of its design to captured German Zeus panzermechs, it is held in high regard by Soviet generals hoping to regain the initiative as the winter thaw begins.

MARCH 1947

As the weather slowly improves, German reconnaissance forces are quick to begin operations to the north of Warsaw, probing aggressively for a soft spot in the Soviet lines. As effective as the Spinnes and armoured recce forces are, the Russian Cossack scout walkers are equal to the task and provide stiff opposition to the German scouts. With no obvious routes open to the north, German attention moves to the south of Warsaw. The morale of Russian forces, at a low prior to the winter, is fractionally improved, having avoided the repeated setbacks that marked the end of 1946. However, Soviet forces in Danzig hover on the brink of defeat and Stalin orders operations

Soviet Ursus troops charge at flimsy enemy defences

to relieve the besieged force – refusing to allow the Germans the satisfaction of defeating them. Striking west from deep staging areas in Minsk and Wilno, the refurbished 1st Guards Tank Army spearheads a major offensive to liberate the Danzig pocket. Pushing west, they hit the German forces in East Prussia hard and quickly force the Germans onto the defensive.

Further south in Czechoslovakia and Yugoslavia, Communist agents work hard to regenerate and resupply the Resistance groups harassing the German garrisons. Results are mixed as the hard winter diminished the fighting will of many soldiers. In Yugoslavia particularly, anti-Communist groups backed by the US are in direct combat with the Soviet-backed guerrillas. Fresh from the training grounds in Berlin, battalions of fanatical SS Shocktroopers are deployed into the Czechoslovakian garrisons; they are both highly effective and brutal in their dealings with the rebel groups.

With little Axis opposition, Soviet forces complete the liberation of Bulgaria and turn west to Greece and Albania. Germany has little option but to surrender ground, but reinforces its position in Turkey to ensure that a threat to the Soviet's flank forces caution. In turn, Turkey walks a dangerous path, utilising German support to protect itself from Russia, whilst being careful not to antagonise Stalin into invading. Despite this careful manoeuvring, confrontation with the Soviet Union appears inevitable.

APRIL 1947

The Soviet 1st Guards Tank Army leads the 1st Belorussian Front westwards, an unstoppable hammer blow aimed straight at Danzig. Despite the best efforts of German defenders, the Soviet forces seem unbeatable but are made to pay heavily for their gains. Soviet Mammoth and Mastodon walkers smash defences whilst Heavy Armoured Infantry secure the territory gained. More traditional forces follow up quickly, providing a defensive mass to deter German counter-attacks. Counter-attacks are made however, and the Luftwaffe is able to gain limited air superiority over a cautious Red Air Force. By the end of April, Soviet forces have reached Danzig and broken the siege but have not yet driven the German forces from the area.

As successful as the operation is, news in Warsaw is less positive: Germany has infiltrated large parts of the city and its terror troops have secured many politically sensitive landmarks. Although there is little left in the city to fight over, the importance of Warsaw to both Stalin and Hitler makes victory necessary for both sides. Stalin is furious at the perceived German success and orders increased efforts to evict them from Warsaw.

The presence of large numbers of SS Shocktroopers in Czechoslovakia has a profound impact on the Resistance groups in the country. No longer sheltered by the population, they are forced into the countryside and become less effective. Soviet efforts to provide additional support are largely fruitless as a network of informers (both willing and unwilling) starts to compromise their ranks.

MAY 1947

The fighting in Warsaw intensifies, as more and more Soviet forces are fed into the shattered city. Reminiscent of Stalingrad, it appears neither side has fully learnt from the earlier experience. Soviet numbers are vast, but German super-soldiers are the perfect answer in the rubble-strewn and largely destroyed city. Shreckwulfen, Totenkorps and Nachtjägers terrorise the mostly conscript Soviet forces,

causing casualties and dismay far in excess of their actual numbers. Around Danzig, having reached their objective, Soviet forces dig in and miss an opportunity to push the Germans further west. As has become normal on the Eastern Front, German forces recover quickly and launch repeated raids behind enemy lines with Falcon droptroopers and terror-causing super-soldiers. The buoyant mood of the Soviet Army in the region is quickly reduced to the nervousness of the preceding year.

German commanders in Czechoslovakia report to Berlin that the Resistance threat is effectively neutralised. In Yugoslavia, US- and Soviet-backed guerrillas continue their war within a war, much to the grim amusement of the German garrisons who are often left unharmed as a result. As frustration in the region grows, President Truman orders the US Paragon Programme to 'deliver him something that can solve the mess in the Balkans'.

With initial operations focussed north in the previous few months, the 2nd Ukrainian Front begins increased operations towards Austria. The Soviet forces in Hungary had suffered a hard winter, in almost constant conflict with the local population. Rough handling of the Hungarian

Fallschirmjäger Falcons emerge from the forest

population has not helped to calm the situation and, as the Soviet forces began moving northwest to the Austrian border, terrorist attacks on their logistic centres delay operations. Rumours of an elite German unit inserted into Budapest to co-ordinate Resistance operations prove impossible to confirm, but the level of sophistication and control exhibited by the guerrillas certainly suggests outside assistance. Despite this, the Soviet juggernaut is poised on the Austrian border and crosses it in early May, swamping the initial defences by weight of numbers. German and Austrian forces quickly retaliate and, having had time to prepare defences in depth, are quick to blunt the Soviet spearhead forces. With the first Soviet efforts repulsed, a carefully planned German counter-offensive quickly cuts off the forward elements of the Soviet Army

and is able to capture two whole divisions that had over extended their advance. Soviet morale in the region drops dramatically, suggesting the impact of the purges the previous year are not fully resolved.

JUNE 1947
This is now...

German heavy panzershreck team

Europe, June 1947

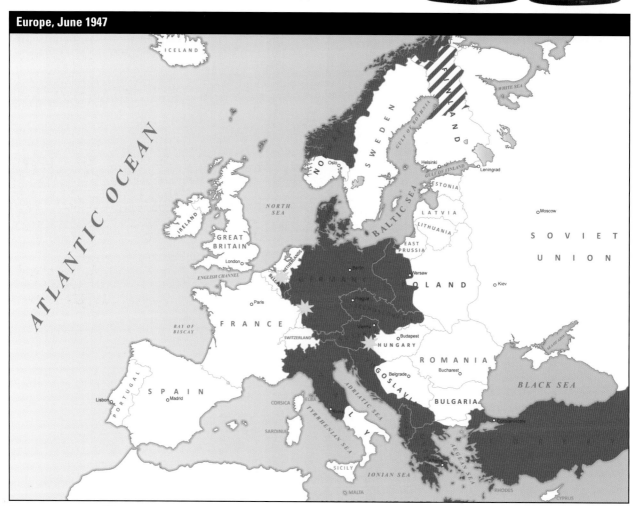

THE MIDDLE EAST AND PERSIAN FRONT

NOVEMBER 1946–FEBRUARY 1947

Although the winter paralysing Europe has less impact on this front, a period of inactivity is forced on the largely mountainous border areas. The difficulties moving supplies from Europe mean that Russia and the Allies are dependent on alternative routes to reinforce their troops. The Soviet forces in the north of Iran are able to consolidate their position, whilst simultaneously reorganising their command structure to conduct operations both in Iran and on the Turkish border. The Allies use the time equally wisely and, having grown from a largely logistical force reinforced in an improvised manner, they have adjusted their organisation into coherent and balanced combat brigades. The US element is brought under a unified, British-led Allied headquarters that now correctly answers to Middle East Command in Cairo. Turkey presses ahead with a limited modernisation of its military under German direction, their air force in particular receiving significantly improved aircraft.

MARCH 1947

As the weather improves and travel through the mountain passes and routes becomes easier, Soviet supplies start heading south to refresh and reinforce their troops in central Iran. The front line follows a line from Tehran, southeast towards Zahedan, following both the railway and the foothills of the Zagros Mountains. The British Commonwealth and their US allies watch the increased Soviet activity from their defensive positions on the higher ground, but with little in the way of new equipment or orders, they can do little but observe. Allied intelligence has few details of the purpose of the Soviet activity, but it is clear that much of the logistical effort is focussed towards the southeast, potentially threatening Zahedan and, presumably, the Allied supply routes to India.

Much Russian political and military activity is also clearly directed at Turkey, as the Soviets become nervous of the increased support being given by Germany. Stalin orders Turkey to evict the German 'advisors' and to join his cause against the German Reich. With the UK and US already fighting on too many fronts, they can offer little support, and certainly less than Germany is already providing. Turkey remains locked in an arrangement with Germany as the threat from the Soviet Union is considered both imminent and real. German efforts over the winter to modernise the Turkish military have been successful in parts, but not universally so. The Turkish Army lacks mechanised forces, but has a huge mobilised infantry force that is ideally suited to the mountainous border regions with Russia and Iran.

Clashes along these borders occur frequently throughout the month but without any major escalations. Opposing Turkish and Soviet forces are content to remind each other of their respective positions without risking major casualties. German requests to open up a sustained front are met with political and military delay as Turkey seeks to postpone full-scale conflict with Russia for as long as possible.

APRIL 1947

The build up of Soviet supplies in central Iran becomes significant enough to force the Allies into action. Deliberate reconnaissance operations are ordered along the whole of the Allied–Soviet front line. Much of this activity is to gather intelligence and is supported by focussed and aggressive air patrols from the RAF and US Air Force. The Soviets are swift to respond and fierce, small-scale encounters become the new norm. With little in the way of reserves, the Allies are careful to ensure that these operations do not escalate beyond their resources, whilst urgent messages are sent to both London and Washington that further efforts are needed to

British Galahad Armoured Infantry

curb Soviet expansion in the Persian Gulf. Britain responds first, diverting more Indian and South African forces to the region at the expense of a frustrated Far Eastern Command. The US also continues to trickle in reinforcements, again, many of which would have gone to the Pacific Theatre. More risky is the US decision to divert war materiel destined for China to their forces in Iran.

Soviet naval activity in the Black Sea steps up, a direct challenge to Turkish control of access to the Mediterranean, and tension between the two regional powers reaches a climax. A small force of German U-Boats passes through Istanbul and into the Black Sea; in response Russia triggers historical claims on much of north eastern Turkey and moves yet more infantry forces to the border. The inevitable clash between Turkey and Russia arrives on 23 April, where Turkish artillery pre-emptively shells Soviet positions across the Soviet and Iranian borders.

MAY 1947

As the border clashes escalate, Soviet forces cross the Turkish border and strike along the coastal road towards Rize. Hopa falls almost immediately to the advancing Russians, but the need to mostly move on foot over rough terrain leads to slow progress. Parallel advances on Ardahan and Kars encounter dug-in defenders that stops Soviet forward progress swiftly. Artillery becomes the weapon of choice with both sides looking for an opening to exploit. German military advisors are sent to the area to assist the Turkish senior officers, but the Turkish generals largely ignore their presence. They do, however, make use of the newly provided German equipment, including Spinne panzermechs and more traditional armoured cars that can operate effectively in the rugged terrain.

In Iran, the Soviet forces continue to stockpile supplies for what is obviously planned to be a significant operation. The alert and observant Allied positions on the higher ground to the south can only watch and wonder as further military aid to the region seems unlikely in the short term. In an effort to glean the Soviet's intent, a series of raids are conducted by US, Indian and British commandos in an attempt to capture Russian prisoners with the appropriate knowledge of their military plans.

British forces in Iraq are put on increased alert and reconnaissance of the Turkish border region is stepped up. In Irbil, stores are stockpiled in case there is a need for extended military operations into either Iran or Turkey.

JUNE 1947

This is now…

THE FAR EAST AND ASIA

NOVEMBER 1946–FEBRUARY 1947

The invasion of Iwo Jima reignites the battle in the Pacific as US Marines seek to exact revenge for their previous defeat on the island. The fighting is as fierce as before, but the US Navy is better prepared for the threat of Japanese submarines, and although their operations are heavily disrupted, the marines on the island receive better and more consistent support.

Although keen to appease US demands for co-ordinated action across the theatre, the British desire to liberate former Commonwealth territory remains paramount. Protracted negotiations are conducted between the Allies as to where best to launch the next major offensive campaign with little to no conclusion. The Soviet Union declares its backing for the Chinese Communist Party (CCP) against the ruling Kuomintang (KMT) government. Whilst clearly enough to potentially undermine US influence in the region, it stops short of declaring war with Japan.

MARCH 1947

Soviet backing of the Chinese Communist Party in northern China results in the creation of training camps and Soviet advisors entering the country. The Chinese government is outraged and demands immediate additional support from the US, who, weary of the continual and inconsistent Chinese demands, are slow to promise anything other than continued logistical and advisor assistance. With an increasing Communist threat in the north, and continued Japanese advances in the east, Chiang Kai-shek's government looks increasingly isolated.

The Soviet Union, although keen to avoid a head on confrontation with Japan, recognise that they have an opportunity to back a force that can curb Japanese expansion in northern China. A modest investment of training personnel, small arms and artillery is enough to influence the direction of the Chinese Communist Party, and encourage their military ambitions against the nationalist KMT government.

The Allies, meanwhile, are locked in frustrated debate over the next steps. The US continues to steadily take ground on

Iwo Jima, and its fall is considered inevitable. Despite this, the US recognises the Japanese mainland is an objective too far with Allied forces hampered at sea and spread thinly over the Pacific Theatre. The British and Australians are keen to secure Australia's northern coastline, considered at risk while Japan has substantial forces in the Dutch East Indies. A further irritant to the Commonwealth is the continued struggle in New Guinea which is sapping Australian morale and proving politically difficult for the government of Australian Prime Minister Chifley. With little clear direction, further Commonwealth forces arrive in New Guinea, including veterans of Wingate's first Chindit campaign, largely replacing the US troops being pulled back from combat operations in the interior. British and Commonwealth forces in Burma are moved south, although no strategic decision is made as to their intended use.

APRIL 1947

The Chinese Communist Party (CCP) escalates the tension within China by attempting an assassination of Chiang Kai-shek. Although unsuccessful, the move confirms the government's belief that the CCP is the greatest threat to China, even more so than the occupying Japanese. The assassination attempt also kills two senior US officers present at the attack. The US increases intelligence and special operations efforts against the CCP and starts to discover the covert hand of the Soviet Union in the organisation. Clashes between Nationalist Chinese forces and Soviet-backed CCP forces occur in the more remote northern provinces and the risk of a costly civil war looms.

Japan seeks to capitalise on the events by initiating small-scale incursions from occupied territory. None are significant in themselves, but each operation occupies another small town or village and the Japanese front line edges westwards. Efforts to mobilise provincial militia are enhanced, with many disenchanted Chinese peasants willing to fight against the discredited Nationalist government; many more flee to the CCP as a preferred alternative. Recognising the need to foster some form of permanent occupation of the Chinese mainland, specific orders are issued to ensure the treatment of former Chinese territories is 'reasonable'. Japan is keen to encourage a civil war in the rest of China, with the US and Soviet Union backing each side, whilst maintaining a 'beneficial' hold on the parts it occupies.

General MacArthur responds to the diversion of supplies to Iran in the strongest manner he can, delaying any further offensive operations until he has the tools to do the job. The lack of Heavy Armoured Infantry is seen as a critical shortfall, particularly when trying to clear dug-in Japanese infantry from fortified positions. With better supply lines through India, Commonwealth forces in Burma push east, both to isolate and

Japanese forces attempt to repel a US beach landing

Japanese Empire, June 1947

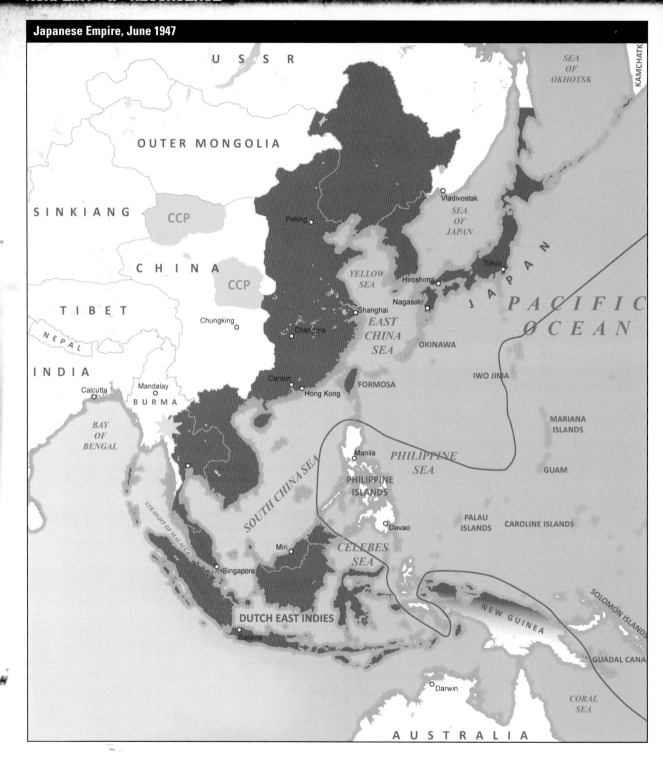

U S S R

OUTER MONGOLIA

SINKIANG

CCP

C H I N A

CCP

T I B E T

NEPAL

INDIA

BURMA

Mandalay

Calcutta

BAY
OF
BENGAL

Chungking

Changma

Shanghai

Peking

Vladivostak

SEA
OF
JAPAN

Hiroshima

Nagasaki

Tokyo

JAPAN

SEA
OF
OKHOTSK

KAMCHATKA

PACIFIC
OCEAN

YELLOW
SEA

EAST
CHINA
SEA

OKINAWA

IWO JIMA

FORMOSA

Canton

Hong Kong

SOUTH CHINA SEA

STRAIGHT OF MALACCA

Singapore

Manila

PHILIPPINE
ISLANDS

PHILIPPINE
SEA

GUAM

MARIANA
ISLANDS

PALAU
ISLANDS

CAROLINE ISLANDS

Davao

Miri

CELEBES
SEA

DUTCH EAST INDIES

Batavia

NEW GUINEA

SOLOMON ISLANDS

GUADAL CANAL

Darwin

CORAL
SEA

A U S T R A L I A

Australian troops withdraw as Japanese Gaikokkaku lead an assault

eventually retake Malaya and Singapore, and to liberate the remaining occupied Burmese territory. This action irritates MacArthur further as he sees it as a waste of precious resources needed further to the east.

MAY 1947

Iwo Jima falls to the exhausted US forces and the capture of the island denies the Japanese a valuable airbase from which to target Allied shipping and naval forces. With the US Marines in need of a significant period of recuperation, the US Army replaces them on the island. However, the threat to the US Navy remains as short-range submarine hunter-killer packs attempt to exact some form of revenge for the defeat. With the US Navy constantly mobile as a result, air cover is not complete and Japanese bombing raids on the islands make the US occupation uncomfortable for the soldiers tasked with fortifying the island. Some much needed Rift-tech supplies begin to arrive in the theatre including a new jet fighter, the P-80 Shooting Star, capable of operating from the US Navy's carriers.

In China, the ruling Nationalist government is reduced to ineffective rhetoric as conflict with the CCP and Japan, and a lack of public support, proves almost overwhelming. With little agreement within the government, the US has little ability to influence Chinese policy and it seems likely China will fracture into several provincial states, falling under the CCP, local Warlords, or the Japanese respectively. Additional US officers are seconded to Chinese training units in an attempt to provide a cadre of reliable and effective formations to strengthen the ailing government. Increasingly nervous after the attempt on his life, Chiang Kai-shek becomes more withdrawn and distrustful of the efforts by outside powers. Fixated on the threat of the CCP, what additional military resources he successfully secures from the Allies is directed against the Communists. The territories occupied by Japan are deemed less critical than the immediate demands of the Nationalist Government's survival.

Commonwealth forces in Burma find themselves facing the Japanese 15th and 33rd Armies that are well supported by the sympathetic Thai (Siamese) forces. Led by the experienced XV Indian Corps, fighting on the Siam–Burma border is inconclusive as the Japanese have no desire to advance back into Burma and the British and Commonwealth forces lack the numbers and mechanical transport to exploit any weaknesses or gaps in the Japanese lines.

In New Guinea, a combined SAS and Commando special operations force discovers and captures a Japanese jungle laboratory that has clearly been using Rift-tech equipment to create their much-feared corpse soldiers. The facility is captured with no survivors and there is little more the commandos can do but to destroy the site, after recovering a few interesting pieces of technology for exploitation in the UK.

JUNE 1947

This is now...

SNLF Trooper

NEW AND REVISED RULES

Since the release of the original rulebook in 2016, there have been countless hours of playtesting conducted by both the team at Clockwork Goblin and by the thousands of players who have leapt into the *Konflikt '47* world. We have also seen the release of a new edition of *Bolt Action* which introduced some interesting rules tweaks to the core *Bolt Action* game engine. As a result, the following section introduces some of the best new rules from earlier *Bolt Action* supplements, the new edition of *Bolt Action* and the *Konflikt '47* writing desk. These additions now form part of the official *Konflikt '47* set of rules.

Imperial Japanese Officer

SUMMARY OF NEW RULES

- Attacking units with differing Damage values or special rules
- New weapons (Compression weapons, Meteor launchers, light Tesla cannons and Schwerefeld Projektors)
- Headquarters rules (Snap to Action, Medic)
- Special rules (Stubborn, Motivate, War Dogs, Hunter)
- Armoured and mechanised platoons and associated rules
- Armoured recovery vehicle rules

SUMMARY OF CHANGES

- Weapon updates (Assault rifle range, LMG and MMG rates of fire, flamethrowers, Tesla weapons)
- Pintle and multiple weapon mounts
- Role of Transports
- Special rules (Fanatic, Flight, Tough Fighter, Jump, Recce)

NEW AND AMENDED COMBAT RULES

With the addition of some specialist units, the need to clarify the procedure for shooting at units with a mixed Damage value is detailed below. We also take the opportunity to adjust some of the weapon characteristics in the core rulebook, and to introduce some completely new weapons!

ATTACKING UNITS WITH DIFFERING DAMAGE VALUES OR SPECIAL RULES

This book introduces some unusual units that may have differing special rules amongst their members, and even mixed experience levels. The units involved are specifically the US Paragon squad, Hauptmann Gross and the Daughters of the Motherland Patriot Team (Commissar Drugov uses a variation of these rules as befits a Hero of the Soviet Union). Other units may be released in the future that also fall into this category. These rules add a level of complexity, but allow the use of more colourful and cinematic units that fit nicely with the *Konflikt '47* game.

When being shot at, the firing player works out how many hits are scored as usual. The defending player can then choose to allocate these hits against his models as normal, but must spread the hits as evenly as possible between models in the target unit. No model may be allocated a second hit until all models in the unit have been hit at least once, and so on if the number of hits requires a model to be hit a third time. If needed, place the hit dice next to the target models if that helps. Once the hits are allocated against the respective models, roll for damage. Any special rules, such as Tough or

Resilient, are then considered after the damage has been determined against each model. If the firer achieves an exceptional damage result, he may reallocate the exceptional damage to any model in the defending unit, which can then use any special rules to avoid the damage if it is able to. If a model receives multiple hits and is removed as a casualty before all the damage from those hits have been resolved, the excess damage is lost and is not transferred to the rest of the target unit.

When firing with weapons of differing PEN values on a target with mixed Damage values or special rules, resolve all the attacks with the same PEN value together (or use different coloured dice) to ensure that the hits scored for each PEN value are allocated clearly.

Example: A unit of 8 Regular Soviet infantry has a Daughters of the Motherland Patriot Team attached to it. The unit suffers 9 hits from incoming fire. The defending player allocates the first 8 hits to the Regular infantry and the ninth to the attached Daughters. Whilst rolling to damage, the Daughter is damaged and fails her Tough check, and one of the hits on the Regular soldiers becomes exceptional damage. The firing player decides to allocate this damage to the other Daughter model. At the end of the shooting, both Daughters are dead and the Regular infantry are feeling a little less secure about their future.

During Close Assault, point-blank fire is conducted using the rules above for shooting. When attacking a unit with differing Damage values or special rules in hand-to-hand combat, the attacking player must apportion the number of attacks to each particular group, type or individual models before rolling to damage. Once damage is determined, the defending player can use any special rules as applicable. Any damage in excess of that needed to remove casualties is lost.

Example: Using the same Soviet unit as detailed above, the attacking unit are rolling 12 damage rolls in hand-to-hand combat. The attacking player could nominate 6 rolls against the Regular infantry and 6 against the Daughters of the Motherland. If the rolls against the Daughters result in more than two kills, any excess damage is lost.

REVISED WEAPONS TABLES

The two tables below provide the latest details of all the weapons currently in use in the game. A couple of changes have been made with the release of this supplement. Notably, assault rifle range is reduced to 18", LMGs and MMGs have an increased number of shots, and flamethrower rules have been revised.

SMALL ARMS WEAPONS TABLE

Type	Range (")	Shots	Pen	Special Rules
Rifle	24	1	-	-
Pistol	6	1	-	Assault
Submachine gun (SMG)	12	2	-	Assault
Shotgun	18	1	-	Assault
Automatic rifle	30	2	-	-
Assault rifle	18	2	-	Assault
Compression rifle	24	3	-1	-
Heavy Tesla rifle (rapid fire mode)	12	3	-	Assault
Light machine gun (LMG)	30	4	-	-
Medium machine gun (MMG)	36	5	-	Team, Fixed
Dual weapon pack	6	2	-	Assault

Japanese forces storm a native village led by a Type 6 Sasori walker

HEAVY WEAPONS TABLE

Type	Range (")	Shots	Pen	Special Rules
Dual weapon pack	18	1	+2	-
Heavy Tesla rifle (single shot mode)	24	1	+1	-
Heavy machine gun (HMG)	36	3	+1	Team, Fixed
Light automatic cannon	48	2	+2	Team, Fixed, HE(D2)
Heavy automatic cannon	72	2	+3	Team, Fixed, HE(D2)
Anti-tank rifle	36	1	+2	Team
PIAT	12	1	+5	Team, Shaped Charge
Bazooka	24	1	+5	Team, Shaped Charge
Super-bazooka	24	1	+6	Team, Shaped Charge
Panzershreck	24	1	+6	Team, Shaped Charge
Panzerfaust	12	1	+6	One-shot, Shaped Charge
Light AT gun	48	1	+4	Team, Fixed, HE(D2)
Medium AT gun	60	1	+5	Team, Fixed, HE(D2)
Heavy AT gun	72	1	+6	Team, Fixed, HE(D3)
Super-heavy AT gun	84	1	+7	Team, Fixed, HE(D3)
Light compression cannon	36	3	+3	Team, Fixed, Compression Wave
Compression cannon	48	3	+4	Team, Fixed, Compression Wave
M21 light Tesla cannon	30	1	+1/+4	Team, Fixed, Tesla
M17 Tesla cannon	36	1	+1/+7	Team, Fixed, Tesla
Flamethrower (Infantry)	6	1 (D6)	+2	Team, Flamethrower
Light flamethrower (Vehicle)	12	1 (D6)	+3	Flamethrower
Flamethrower (Vehicle)	12	1 (D6+1)	+3	Flamethrower
Rifle grenade	6-18	1	HE	Indirect Fire, HE (D2)
Light mortar	12-24	1	HE	Team, Indirect Fire, HE(D3)
Medium mortar	18-60	1	HE	Team, Fixed, Indirect Fire, HE(D6)
Heavy mortar	18-72	1	HE	Team, Fixed, Indirect Fire, HE(2D6)
Light howitzer	0/24-48	1	HE	Team, Fixed, Indirect Fire, HE(D6)
Medium howitzer	0/24-60	1	HE	Team, Fixed, Indirect Fire, HE(2D6)
Heavy howitzer	0/24-72	1	HE	Team, Fixed, Indirect Fire, HE(3D6)
Meteor launcher	60	1D6	+4	Team, Fixed, Meteor Strike
Zvukovoy Proyektor	24	Special	Special	Team, Fixed, Shockwave
Light Schwerefeld Projektor	36	2	+3	Team, Fixed, Gravity Pulse
Schwerefeld Projektor	48	2	+4	Team, Fixed, Gravity Pulse

TYPES OF WEAPON

Compression weapons. The Japanese have refined elements of Germany's Rift-tech research into gravity energy and gravitic waves and have produced a new range of weapons based on the advances they have uncovered. The compression cannon appears to work on the bonding between molecules and can compress and expand these bonds to produce excessive strain and resultant damage to objects. The cannon fires alternating pulses of energy that effectively rip a target apart at the molecular level. Heavy armour can act as a barrier in so far as it absorbs the damage, but is left weakened and damaged after receiving fire. Softer materials can be partially

IJA Ghost Suit

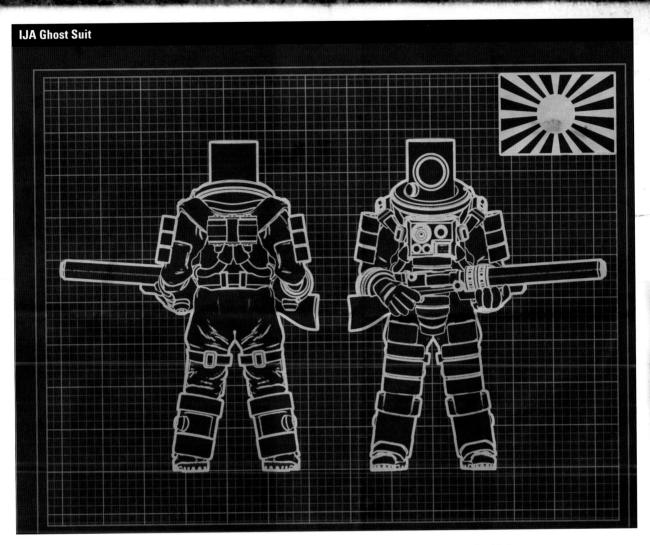

disintegrated by a sustained blast. Lighter versions of the cannon have been produced, including small arms for their Rift-tech equipped infantrymen, although this version of the technology lacks the raw damage potential of its larger cousins.

Meteor launcher. The Meteor launcher is a rocket-launching system that includes an experimental Rift-tech-based chemical core within each of the rockets fired. The chemicals are designed to degrade metals, are fast acting, and in enough quantity can weaken the integrity of a vehicles armour, allowing the other rockets in the salvo to penetrate more easily. Over a longer time period, the enzymes can turn hardened steel into a brittle honeycomb that can be broken by hand, but the time taken for that is far longer than the length of a typical engagement. Launchers of varying sizes have been trialled, with a view to fitting them to different turrets and

therefore different armoured vehicles.

WEAPON SPECIAL RULES

With the addition of these two new weapon types, the following rules explain how they are used in the game. Also included are some revised rules to represent changes to the way flamethrowers and Tesla weapons work.

Light Machine Guns

Under the description of team weapons in the core rulebook, LMGs are unfortunately cited as an example of team weapons within infantry squads. However, LMGs do not have the Team Weapon special rule and are therefore not Team Weapons with regard to the Team Weapon rules as presented on page 63 of the *Konflikt '47* rulebook. However, when purchased as part of an infantry squad, a member of that squad may be required to act as the loader as indicated by the weapon option in the unit entry. If a loader is not available (usually due to casualties), the weapon fires at a -1 to hit penalty in the same way as a Team Weapon.

Loaders

The loader of a weapon such as an LMG, light mortar or heavy Tesla rifle ensures the weapon maintains a steady rate of fire and provides fresh ammunition and new barrels or fuel cells as required. If a unit entry in the force list states that a loader is required for a particular weapon option, one of the members of the unit is nominated as the loader and may not fire its own weapon when the heavier weapon is fired. Troop entries that do not include the requirement for a loader do not need to nominate a loader from the squad (British Galahad squads for example). If a loader is required but is not available, the weapon shoots at -1 to hit.

Finnish Flamethrower Team

Flamethrower (Revised)

Flamethrowers never suffer the 'to hit' penalties for cover or if the target is Down. This makes flamethrowers especially effective against troops in bunkers or behind cover, as well as troops lying flat on the ground (which is not a good defence against flaming liquids being sprayed at you!). When shooting a flamethrower, roll a single dice to hit. If you score a hit then the number of hits is multiplied into D6 (infantry or light flamethrower) or D6+1 (vehicle flamethrower). Roll for damage in the usual manner.

Flamethrowers always hit the top armour of vehicles – this represents the tendency of burning liquid to seep through hatches and other openings. Also, flamethrowers don't rely on kinetic energy to penetrate a target's armour, so they don't suffer the -1 PEN penalty when firing at long range.

The Gun Shield rule (rulebook, page 88) does not apply when shooting at artillery targets with a flamethrower. The Extra Protection rule (rulebook, page 109) does not apply when shooting at targets inside buildings with a flamethrower. In both cases, neither building nor gun shield offers any additional protection against a flamethrower.

Any unit hit by a flamethrower takes 1 pin marker because it has been hit, and a further D3 pin markers to account for the unbridled terror unleashed upon it, for a total of D3+1 pin markers on the target.

If a unit is hit by a flamethrower, it must always check its morale once firing has been worked out and pin markers allocated as described above. Note that a morale check is required regardless of the number of casualties caused and even if no damage has been suffered at all. A unit failing this check is destroyed immediately – its morale completely shattered. Vehicles failing their morale in this way are abandoned and considered destroyed.

After shooting with an infantry man-pack flamethrower, roll a D6. On a result of 1, the flamethrower has run out of fuel and is now useless. If this happens, the entire flamethrower team is removed as if it had fallen casualty. Although this might seem harsh it does reflect the extreme risks run by troops carrying flamethrowers and introduces a level of unpredictability that balances the weapon's effectiveness.

After shooting with a vehicle-mounted flamethrower, roll a D6 (or a dice for each flamethrower if the vehicle has more than one). On a result of 1, that flamethrower has run out of fuel and is now useless. This does not otherwise affect the vehicle.

When rolling on the damage effects chart against a vehicle equipped with flamethrowers, add an extra +1 to the roll to represent the increased risk from carrying around so much volatile fuel for the flamethrower.

Compression Wave

When firing a compression weapon (except compression rifles), roll to hit normally for its three shots. It does damage at the appropriate PEN value for each shot following the normal rules for multi-shot weapons. However, if all three shots hit the target, apply the following secondary effects before rolling to damage, and for this attack only:

COMPRESSION WAVE	
Target	**Effect**
Infantry	Roll an additional 3 'to hit' rolls.
Artillery	Roll D6, 1–4 treat as infantry, 5–6 gun destroyed
Vehicle	Roll an additional 'to hit' roll
Building	No effect

Tesla (Revised)

Tesla weapons have two PEN values, the lower value is used against infantry and artillery and the higher value is used against vehicles. Penetration is not reduced when firing at long range.

When targeting infantry and artillery, the weapon arcs to nearby targets. After a successful hit is rolled, roll a D6, this number of additional hits is inflicted on the unit. If the number of hits exceeds the number of models in the unit, any excess hits are lost.

Meteor Strike

The Meteor launcher fires a number of small rockets, each with a ceramic warhead holding the metal-degrading enzyme and a tungsten core at the centre of the rocket. Determine the number of shots on target by rolling 1D6 as indicated in the Shots column of the Weapons Table. Then roll to hit for each shot as normal. For infantry and artillery, this is the number of hits; roll to damage using the base PEN value shown on the Weapons Table. For vehicles, the PEN value of the weapon is equal to the PEN value on the table, +1 for each successful hit. Roll a single damage roll at this modified PEN value.

NEW HEADQUARTERS SPECIAL RULES

The following rules are added to the section regarding Headquarters units; the role of officers has been enhanced. This better justifies their cost with regard to points, and makes them central to seizing the initiative or executing a plan, as befits their true-life significance.

going on to the next. Note that units ordered this way still need to take order tests as normal if they are pinned, and clearly can't be given an order dice if they already have one. Officers in reserve cannot use this special rule.

Example: An American First Lieutenant is ordered to Run. His unit has two pin markers, so it must take an order test first. The test is passed, so the player places the order die showing Run next to the officer. He then draws two more of his order dice from the bag and assigns them to a Firefly squad and an artillery unit that are within 6", ordering the Fireflies to Rally and the artillery piece to Fire. The order dice are placed next to the two units showing the relevant orders. Then the player fires with the artillery. Then he takes the Rally test with the Firefly squad, and finally Runs the officer's unit. He could have resolved these three orders in any sequence once the orders had been allocated.

OFFICERS

The following rule is added to all officers, thereby allowing them to have a direct and focussed impact on the battlefield. Use of this rule introduces another tactical consideration beyond the decision to include more senior officers in your force. By gaining the momentum at one point of the battle, you risk losing it elsewhere as the number of order dice yet to be drawn will potentially swing in your opponent's favour. This is therefore an interesting and potentially risky decision to make.

Snap to Action

When a Second Lieutenant receives an order successfully (either because no test was required or because of a successful order test) other than Down, you can immediately take one of your order dice from the bag and give an order to a single friendly unit within 6" – you can measure to see which of your units are within 6" before you take dice out of the bag. A First Lieutenant can take up to two dice to give orders to up to two friendly units, a Captain can take three and a Major can take four. Captains and Majors can do this within a range of 12" rather than 6".

Allocate each of the order dice before resolving any orders tests or actions. Once all the drawn order dice have been allocated, they can be activated in any order (including the officer's original order), finishing each unit's action before

MEDICS

In addition to the rules in the core rulebook, Medics may not fire weapons or assault, but can defend themselves if assaulted using point-blank fire if armed, or hand-to-hand combat otherwise. Medic units cannot be used to control or contest objectives in scenarios.

*Imperial Japanese
Army battle exoskeleton*

NEW UNIT SPECIAL RULES

Many units share special rules as indicated in the Army Lists. Further specific rules are included in the entries of individual units where appropriate. The following rules are either additional rules to those presented in the core rulebook, or are revisions to existing rules following player and playtesting feedback.

FANATICS (REVISED)

Fanatics are unwilling to give in and will die fighting rather than flee or surrender. When a Fanatic unit loses half its numbers from enemy fire it does not take a morale check, it continues to fight as normal so long as it includes at least two men. Should the unit be reduced to a single man he must take checks as normal. When a Fanatic unit wins in close-quarter combat, it must always opt for a follow-on round of combat.

FLIGHT (REVISED)

Units that have the Flight special rule move around the battlefield in long leaps, swoops or bounds. They do not stay airborne like aircraft, nor can they hover or manoeuvre freely at altitude. The rule is intended to provide movement options for troops with enhanced mobility such as Nachtjägers and US Firefly jumptroops. The ability to move swiftly whilst ignoring terrain is of great help to infantry that need to cover ground quickly whilst under fire. In some cases, however, the extra attention such movement may attract can be tactically counter-productive!

Units with the Flight rule may move up to 12" when Advancing and 18" when Running. Flying troops may ignore any terrain restrictions on their movement, but must not end their flight in impassable terrain. If Ambushed whilst using their Flight movement they count as in the open and cannot claim cover. Infantry with the Flight rule may elect to move as normal infantry at the start of their activation, in which case they follow all normal rules for infantry movement.

HUNTERS

The most experienced and dangerous snipers and marksmen have often perfected the art of stealthy movement into concealed firing positions. Units with this special rule may conduct an Advance order as normal, but may change the order dice to Ambush instead of firing on the completion of their move. Should the unit fire as an Ambush reaction, it does not count as moving; however, you cannot use the Sniper special rule in the same turn as you use the Hunter special rule (assume the movement and adoption of a new fire position denies the sniper the time to properly prepare his shot).

MOTIVATE

Exceptional officers and leaders are able to maximise the performance of those around them. When a model or unit with this special rule is allocated an order dice, it may select one other activated infantry or artillery unit within 6" and remove the order dice from that unit and place it back in the dice bag. The selected unit can therefore be activated again later in the turn. This does allow an officer to motivate a nearby unit and then immediately allocate it a new order using the Snap to Action rules.

STUBBORN

Stubborn troops don't give in easily! If forced to take a morale check, they ignore negative morale modifiers from pin markers. Remember that order tests and reaction tests are not morale checks.

TOUGH FIGHTERS (REVISED)

Some troops excel at close-quarters fighting, whether because of special selection or training, like commando units, or due to their cultural disposition, as in the case of Ghurkhas and some other colonial troops. When a model with this special rule scores a casualty in hand-to-hand fighting against enemy infantry or artillery units, it can immediately make a second damage roll (but not a third if the second damage roll also scores a kill!). For example, ten Tough Fighters attack in hand-to-hand fighting against a unit of Regular infantry. They roll ten dice to damage and score five casualties. This allows them to immediately roll another five dice to damage, and this time they score two more casualties, for a total of seven casualties. Note that Tough Fighter does not apply to point-blank shooting, just hand-to-hand combat.

WAR DOGS

Several nations have turned to trained canine units to provide specialist capabilities on the battlefield. The addition of Rift-tech developments in genetic manipulation have broadened the utility of the dog in a combat environment. Most notably, the British have developed fighting dogs specifically trained to tackle the fearsome German Totenkorps, and to roam ahead of the front line to disrupt the enemy. Handlers are required to ensure the war dogs are released safely and at the correct time (and in the right direction).

War Dogs are classed as infantry and follow normal infantry rules for movement, orders, combat, etc. At the start of any

IJA Type 6 Ke-Ho 'Sasori'

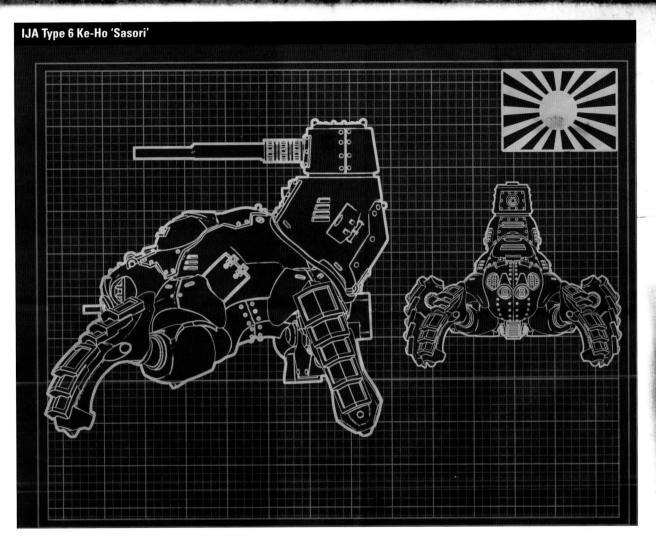

activation that the unit is given a Run (or assault) order, the controlling player can choose to release the dogs. Remove any handler models remaining in the squad from the table (these may not return but do not count as casualties). From this point, the unit is immune to Horror and gains the Fast, Fanatics and Tough Fighter special rules. As the order has already been declared, the dogs follow the order for the remainder of the turn, including direction of movement and target of the assault (if applicable).

However, on subsequent turns, and at the start of any activation where there are no handlers in the unit, a unit of dogs without handlers will always Run towards the nearest infantry or artillery unit when activated. This may include friendly troops unfortunate enough to be in their range. If two units are equally close, enemy units are selected before friendly ones; if both are from the same side, roll a die for each unit, with the lowest roll deemed to be the closest. Units behind impassable terrain are ignored if the dog's movement cannot bring them in to contact. If the Run move would bring the dogs in to contact with the nearest unit, the Run order is changed to an assault and the war dogs conduct an assault instead.

Imperial Japanese Army anti-tank rifle team

VEHICLE RULES

A couple of the existing core vehicle rules are clarified below to better represent the more complicated nature of many of the *Konflikt '47* vehicles. Also, with the introduction later in this book of the option to field mechanised or armoured platoons centred on armoured fighting vehicles rather than infantry, a number of vehicle-specific rules have been added to give a greater feel of armoured combat.

VEHICLE FACING AND ARCS

The facing and arc rules introduced in the core rulebook (page 94) remain extant, however the following revisions are provided to clarify some of the more unusual weapon mounts.

Pintle-mounted Weapons (Revised)

Some vehicles carry one or more machine guns on a swivelling type of mount. These pintle-mounted weapons were commonly fitted to softskins such as jeeps and trucks, as well as to armoured carriers. They were also fitted on top of armoured vehicles for defence against low-level air attack; however, they were inevitably used against ground targets when the opportunity arose. Depending on where they are mounted, a pintle-mounted gun can cover anywhere from a single arc to 360-degree as noted in the vehicle's description. If a pintle-mounted weapon is on a turret, it has a 360-degree arc of fire.

Whenever a fully enclosed armoured vehicle fires a pintle-mounted weapon against a ground target, the crew are exposing themselves to enemy small-arms fire, and thus the vehicle counts as open-topped until the end of the turn. Mark such vehicle with an appropriate token. Pintle-mounted machine guns can be fired against aircraft and therefore have the Flak special rule (see page 79). Note that when firing a pintle-mounted machine gun against an aircraft, fully enclosed vehicles do not count as open-topped. Note that there are a few cases of vehicles that were designed so that the crew could fire pintle-mounted weapons safely from inside the vehicle (in which case this last rule does not apply) – this will be specified in the vehicle's entry.

Multiple Weapons, Linked Weapons and Multiple Mounts

When the structure of the vehicle and the way the weapons are mounted make it very obvious that a weapon system consists of multiple weapons on the same mount, or multiple barrels firing at a single target (such as, for example, the four HMGs of an American M16 anti-aircraft carriage, or the two HMGs and autocannon in a Kodiak assault walker arm mount), all of those weapons must be fired at the same target. Only

Totenkorps being moved to the frontlines

weapons on separate mounts can split fire; for example, you could fire the co-axial machine gun or main gun of a Sherman against one target, the hull-mounted machine gun against a separate (or the same) target, and the pintle-mounted .50 cal on the turret against another (or the same) target.

When firing a multiple weapon mount, each weapon fires its respective number of shots. For example, the Kodiak mentioned above rolls three dice to hit for each of the two HMGs, and then two dice for the light autocannon, so a total of eight dice are rolled for each arm, and the left and right arms may target separate targets if they wish.

If a mount has several weapons using the HE special rule (you cannot decide that some of these weapons fire armour-piercing and some fire HE, they must all fire the same type of ammunition), roll to hit and then determine the effects of each HE hit separately, noting the rules on multiple HE hits on vehicles of course!

Some weapons are described as 'linked' in the vehicles unit entry; these weapons are considered to be on the same mount, even if physically separated on the model. The US Mudskipper's autocannons are a good example of this situation. The autocannons must fire at the same target as if they were on the same mount.

ROLE OF TRANSPORTS (REVISED)

The role of transport vehicles is to carry troops, and once they have arrived in the combat zone their job is done. Some transports are equipped with fire-support weapons such as machine guns, but even so they are not assault vehicles and their crews would not expect to find themselves face to face with the enemy.

To represent this, all empty transports that end the turn closer to an enemy unit of any kind than to a friendly unit, aside from other empty transports, are automatically removed from the battle and count as destroyed. We assume their crews abandon them or else they are driven rapidly away from the action and do not return.

Transport vehicles have a minimal crew but are considered able to fire one of the weapons the vehicle is equipped with. If the vehicle is equipped with more than one weapon, any weapon after the first can only be fired if the vehicle is carrying/towing a unit whose members can act as weapon crew – each weapon being fired needs one man to operate it. If either the vehicle crew or the passengers are Inexperienced, or have a pin markers, their shots suffer the normal penalties, so first declare which weapon is operated by the crew and which by the passengers.

If a vehicle has a transport/tow capacity, but it is not included in the transport and tows section of the force list (for example, if it's in the self-propelled artillery section), both of the rules above do not apply to it.

ARMOURED RECOVERY

Armoured recovery vehicles (ARV) were highly specialised machines with equally specialised crews. They were tasked with keeping fighting vehicles in combat, and recovering those that had broken down and been damaged. A dangerous task, but a vital one nonetheless. An ARV is a dedicated engineering vehicle designed to rescue damaged combat vehicles and may be included in your force outside of any limits on vehicle numbers.

Obviously, only units with the ARV special rule count as ARVs. You may select no more than one ARV for every two vehicles in your force with a Damage value of 8+ (7+ for walkers), paying their requisition points cost for each ARV as normal.

ARVs can be used to recover vehicles with a Damage value of 8 or greater (7 or greater if a walker), lighter vehicles would not be worthy of the risk to the ARV. To tow a vehicle, the ARV must use an Advance order to get into contact with the debilitated vehicle, or begin its activation in contact with it. The ARV must then pass an order test. This is in addition to any test needed to receive the order dice upon activation.

If it fails, nothing happens; the crew are still trying to hook up or free the vehicle, or are waiting for an opportunity in the battle to get out and assess the situation.

If successful, the ARV crew has attached the stricken vehicle. Place the ARV next to the stricken vehicle, in contact with it and on the side nearest your table edge. The ARV should also be facing towards your table edge at this point. While the ARV is towing or carrying a vehicle it may not be given a Run order. Also if it fails an order test or morale check, it has lost control of the damaged vehicle and must reattach itself as described above. Move the two vehicles 1" apart to indicate this. You may also voluntarily stop towing a vehicle by separating the two models at the end of any of the ARV's activations; separate the models as above.

If the ARV touches your table edge whilst towing a vehicle, remove them both from the table, the ARV may not return but does not count as a casualty. If it was towing a friendly vehicle, your opponent loses any victory points they received for that vehicle. At the end of a game, if an ARV is towing a friendly vehicle but is still on the board, your opponent loses half the associated attrition or victory points for the damaged vehicle.

If you manage to tow an enemy's knocked out vehicle off the table, you receive its victory or attrition points for a second time. Likewise if caught on the table at the end of the game towing an enemy vehicle, you receive half of its victory or attrition points again.

Comment: In reality, this dramatically oversimplifies the task of recovering armoured vehicles in combat but adds an interesting modelling and cinematic option to games. Likewise, relative sizes and weights of the towing and towed vehicles have not been factored in for the sake of cinematic licence.

NEW VEHICLE SPECIAL RULES

Many vehicles share special rules as indicated in the Army Lists. Further specific rules are included in the entries of individual units where appropriate. The following rules are revisions to those presented in the core rulebook; both the Flight and Recce special rules require further detail to improve their use on the gaming table.

Jump (Revised)

The US have pioneered heavy repulsors using Rift-technology to allow their walkers to operate as jump-capable vehicles. Whilst not as versatile as the infantry versions, it allows the walkers to navigate through hazardous terrain and clear intervening obstacles and troops.

Vehicles with the Jump special rule ignore terrain when making a jump move, so are always considered to be in open terrain (including if shot at from Ambush) when jumping. Once the vehicle's jump move is completed, the vehicle may benefit from cover as normal. A vehicle with the Jump special rule may also move over intervening models so long as it has enough movement to clear the troops and can land over 1" from any nearby unit.

To conduct a jump, the vehicle must be given a Run order. All jump movement is conducted at the vehicle's Run movement rate and must be in a straight line – no turns are permitted either before or after the jump move. As it has received a Run order, the vehicle may not fire, as per the normal Run order rules.

Recce (Revised)

This special rule normally applies to scout cars, light armoured vehicles and light walkers operating in a scouting, recon or recce (short for reconnaissance) role. Recce vehicles advance ahead of a formation to probe out the enemy's defences – as such they are highly aware of any enemy presence and prepared to avoid trouble. The Recce rule is indicated in the unit entry of the force lists, a vehicle with the Recce special rule loses the rule whilst towing or carrying passengers, but can regain the rule once it stops towing or the passengers disembark.

Once per turn, a vehicle with the Recce rule is allowed to react to an enemy shooting or assaulting them by making a special Recce reaction. The player can choose to do this whether the vehicle has already taken an action that turn or not. A reaction test must be made as normal when the shooting or assault is declared. If the test is failed the vehicle may attempt another recce move later in the turn.

A Recce reaction is a move at Advance or Run rate, which may be forward or reverse, so long as this results in the escaping vehicle ending out of sight of the attacking enemy, or in cover from the attack, or at least further away from the attacker than when the attack is declared. In other words, this move cannot be used to move closer to the attacker. It also cannot be used to assault an enemy unit. Once the escape move is done, mark the vehicle as Down. The enemy's shot is then resolved as normal. If the target has moved out of range or sight then the unit shoots and automatically misses.

When an enemy unit declares an assault against a recce vehicle the vehicle may react with a Recce reaction as described above. If the recce vehicle decides not to attempt a Recce reaction it may instead attempt a Stand and Shoot or Escape reaction as normal if it is able to. After the Recce move is done, measure the range from the assaulting unit. If the unit is out of range, the assaulting unit must simply Run towards the vehicle in its new location. If the assault succeeds, the assault is resolved as normal (assaulting infantry hits on 6, even if the reverse move was done at Run speed).

When attacking, if a target of a recce vehicle is successful in making a Firefight or Stand and Shoot reaction, the recce vehicle may not elect to attempt a Recce move reaction to that response; instead it continues its previous order.

Some recce vehicles can reverse at their Run rate if they are especially small and manoeuvrable or if they have dual-direction steering, as did some German armoured cars. These exceptions are indicated in the force lists. If they fail an order test or are forced to flee for any reason, these vehicles will always reverse at a Run rate.

Recce vehicles will also spot hidden enemy at longer ranges than other vehicles – as noted in the rules for hidden units.

British Cromwell T

FORCE SELECTION AND ARMOURED PLATOONS

For those wishing to use a more vehicle- or walker-orientated force, the rules for fielding an armoured, walker or mechanised platoon are detailed below, including a sample scenario designed for their use.

ARMOURED AND MECHANISED PLATOONS

Although *Konflikt '47* is predominantly an infantry-based game, it can be played enjoyably with armoured forces. Whilst the vehicle combat rules lack the detail and sophistication of a game dedicated to armoured warfare, they can provide an engaging and enjoyable alternative to the standard infantry battles. As such, the following rules allow you to field a mechanised platoon of tanks, walkers or vehicles instead of the normal reinforced infantry platoon structure. Make sure your opponent is aware that you will be fielding an armoured or mechanised platoon and agrees to this – facing an armoured platoon without any preparation is not an enjoyable experience!

To field an armoured or mechanised platoon, use the following Reinforced Armoured Platoon Table to construct your force.

REINFORCED ARMOURED OR MECHANISED PLATOON	
1	Command vehicle from Tank, Tank destroyer, Assault gun, Walker, Armoured car.
2	Vehicles from Tank, Tank destroyer, Assault gun, Walker, Self-propelled artillery, Anti-aircraft vehicle, Armoured car.
Plus	
0–2	Vehicles from Tank, Tank destroyer, Assault gun, Walker, Self-propelled artillery, Anti-aircraft vehicle, Armoured car.
0–3	Infantry squads
0–1	First Lieutenant or Second Lieutenant
0–1	Captain or Major (per force not platoon)
0–1	Medic
0–1	Forward Observer
0–1	Machine gun team
0–1	Mortar team
0–1	Sniper team
0–1	Flamethrower team
0–1	Anti-tank teams
0–1	Field artillery or anti-tank gun
Plus	
0+	Transport for all infantry and artillery units

A command vehicle is simply any of the vehicles available in your national force lists, which has the Command Vehicle special rule. If the vehicle does not have the Command Vehicle rule, it can be purchased for +25pts to allow the vehicle to act as the commander of the platoon.

The armoured or mechanised platoon must have motorised transport for all of its infantry and artillery units, up to a maximum of one transport per unit of infantry/artillery. The only units that are an exception to this, and which cannot have transports, are motorbike infantry and infantry with the flight special rule; these can be included in an armoured or mechanised platoon without additional transport vehicles.

US Bruin walker

SPECIAL RULES FOR ARMOURED PLATOONS

The following special rules only apply to armoured or mechanised platoons; they are not available to vehicles purchased as part of a normal reinforced platoon.

Command Vehicle

A vehicle with the Command Vehicle special rule acts in the same way as an infantry officer. Vehicles with this rule may add a +1 bonus when rolling morale tests to any vehicle within the force that are within its 12" command range. A Command Vehicle may not use the Snap to Action rule, which is specific to infantry and artillery formations.

Radio Networks

Radio networks allow a platoon commander to communicate with individual tanks, walkers and vehicles within the same platoon, and to receive orders from more senior commanders at company or battalion level. To represent the advantages of an effective radio network, the following rule can be used.

If the three compulsory vehicles in the platoon are from the same unit entry in the force lists, then the player can declare they have a Radio Network. The Radio Network adds one to the command vehicle's morale bonus when adding its bonus to any armoured vehicle that forms part of the same platoon. The Radio Network costs an additional +5pts, added to the command vehicle's points cost. So a Command Vehicle with a Radio Network adds +2 to the morale of vehicles from the same platoon that are within 12".

Note that the three compulsory vehicles can have different options or upgrades if relevant, they must however be from the same unit entry. So a US player could take three Sherman tanks, and upgrade one to have the howitzer in place of the 76mm gun, for example.

Senior Command Vehicle

If using more than one armoured or mechanised platoon in your force, you may wish to purchase a Senior Command Vehicle, representing the company or battalion commander. A Senior Command Vehicle must have the Command Vehicle special rule and can add +3 to the morale values of vehicles in the whole force that are within 12". This special rule costs an additional +15pts. A Senior Command Vehicle may not use the Snap to Action rule, which is specific to infantry and artillery formations.

A German Zeus heavy panzermech leads a counter attack against a US advance

PLAYING GAMES WITH ARMOURED OR MECHANISED PLATOONS

The requisition points are still determined by both players as normal; it will largely depend on the time available for the game. With the late/post-war setting of *Konflikt '47*, many of the vehicles are more expensive in terms of requisition points, so a larger game total may be needed to allow for second platoons if desired. 1,500 points will give an enjoyable game, but 1,750 or 2,000 points may be needed to incorporate some of the heaviest vehicles available in the force lists.

Preparing the Battlefield

When using armoured or mechanised vehicles and walkers, the ranges of their weapons will often mean that they can reach across most of an average-sized wargames table. To ensure there is a reasonable amount of manoeuvre in the game, enough terrain should be placed to restrict and block clear lines of sight, particularly across the width of the table. There is no real limit on the amount of terrain needed, a game of armoured walkers fighting in a ruined city would be both accurate and appropriate.

ARMOURED PLATOON SCENARIO

The following scenario is presented as an example of how an armoured platoon game may be played. It can be used as a base for players to adjust as they see fit. Some scenarios may require infantry to secure objectives under armoured escort, or may involve moving through or onto an area of terrain. This scenario focuses on securing multiple objectives on the tabletop, ensuring players must manoeuvre their vehicles to win, not just hide behind cover and shoot!

Set Up Objectives

You will need five objective markers (approx. 1" or 25mm diameter tokens. Spare miniature bases are ideal; if they are decorated with crates, fuels cans, piles of ammo, etc., even better). Both players roll a dice; the highest scorer places the first objective counter anywhere on the table more than 6" from any edge. The other player then places an objective counter at least 18" away from any other counter and more than 6" from a table edge. Players continue to alternate

placing the markers under the same conditions until all are placed. If some adjustment is required to ensure that all five counters can be placed, this can be done by mutual consent.

Roll for Sides

Both players roll a die, the highest scorer may select which table edge he will deploy from; his opponent deploys from the opposite edge (this may be a short edge if players wish).

Prepare Forces

No units are set up on the table at the start of the game. Both sides must nominate at least half of their force to form their first wave. This can be the entire force if desired. Any units not included in the first wave are left in reserve (see page 122 of Konflikt '47 rulebook).

Objectives

Players are trying to capture as many objectives as possible. To capture an objective you must have one of your units within 6" of the objective token at the end of a turn, and there must be no enemy units within 6" of it. At the end of each turn, a player scores a victory point for each objective captured in that turn. Vehicles with the transport rule may not capture objectives, nor may artillery.

First Turn

During Turn 1, both players must bring their first wave onto the table from any point on their starting table edge, and each unit must be given either an Advance or Run order. No order test is required to bring on units in the first wave.

Game Duration

Keep a count of how many turns have elapsed as the game is played. At the end of Turn 7, roll a die. On a result of 1, 2 or 3 the game ends, on a roll of 4, 5 or 6 play one further turn.

Victory!

At the end of the game, total the number of victory points accumulated for each player; the highest total is the winner. In the event of a draw, the winner is the player that has destroyed the most vehicles with a Damage value of 7+ or greater. If still tied, then it's a draw.

Japanese Type 6 Ke Ho recce crawler

NEW UNITS

The following pages contain new unit entries for each of the four nations introduced in the *Konflikt '47* rulebook. These new forces are designed to add further Weird War options to the existing lists and the emphasis has been to develop these new units in preference to more historically based units. In a couple of cases, units from the original rulebook have been reprinted here to take account of the errata that has been issued since the release of the rules.

GERMANY

These additional units may be fielded in a German force in line with the normal force selection rules. As the conflict builds momentum after the savage winter of 1946, the race to perfect Rift-tech weapons and advantages continues. The German's industrial capacity is enhanced with several Rift-tech inspired solutions to key shortages, and new soldiers are being equipped with weaponry and technology thought to be the stuff of fantasy a few years before. Technology gifted to Japan in the previous two years is now returning to the Reich, enhanced and developed in ways the German scientists had not considered. The resurgence of the Axis is inevitable.

ARMY SPECIAL RULES
Hitler's Buzzsaw (Revised)
German units equipped with light and medium machine guns fire one extra shot (five for an LMG and six for an MMG). This includes weapons mounted on vehicles.

HEADQUARTERS UNITS
Heavy Armour Platoon Officer
As the Germans expanded their use of the new Rift-tech developed Heavy Infantry Armour, whole units have been equipped in armoured divisions to form heavy Panzergrenadier forces able to support heavy tank and panzermech battalions. These heavy formations would often be the spearhead of an advance to maximise the damage inflicted on defending forces. Officers of these units would be equipped with the same armour as their troops, although often carried lighter weapons more suited to personal protection. The officer can be accompanied by up to two assistants to run messages and maintain communications back to Battalion HQ.

Germans patrolling a bleak forest

Cost	- Second Lieutenant (Leutnant) 80pts (Veteran) - First Lieutenant (Oberleutnant) 105pts (Veteran) - Captain (Hauptmann) 140pts (Veteran) - Major (Major) 180pts (Veteran)
Team	1 officer and up to 2 further men
Weapons	SMG (officer), assault rifles (men)
Options	- The officer may be accompanied by up to 2 men at a cost of +20pts per man (Veteran). - 1 man may be equipped with a panzerfaust in addition to his assault rifle for +5pts.
Special Rules	- Resilient - Slow - Large Infantry - Must have two Heavy Armoured Infantry squads in the platoon to field this unit.

Hauptmann Heinrich Gross

SS Hauptman Gross is a rising star in the SS Shocktrooper brigades, and as such has been able to assemble his own command group of specialists to enhance his company command and maximise his unit's impact on the battlefield. Hauptmann Gross has been the subject of a number of experimental Rift-tech enhancements that remain shrouded in secrecy, but it is clear there is something more than human about him. His ability to inspire his men is almost supernatural and he is rumoured to possess superior strength, speed and toughness. His reputation as a bestial and bloodthirsty fighter has certainly been earned the hard way at the front line. Hauptmann Gross is also a ruthless and clinical tactician, not averse to sacrificing those around him in pursuit of his goal of leading Germany to ultimate victory.

Cost	265pts (Veteran)
Team	Captain (Gross), Medic (Flount), Sniper (Deitner), and 2 SS Shocktroopers
Weapons	SMG (Gross), rifle (Deitner), assault rifle (Troopers)
Special Rules	- Tough - Fanatic - IR Vision - Sniper (Deitner only) - Medic (Flount only) - Motivate (Gross only) - Fast (Gross only) - Blood-fuelled (Gross only, gains Resilient and Strong for remainder of game if Gross kills an enemy model in hand-to-hand combat)

INFANTRY SQUADS
Waffen-SS Shocktrooper Squad (Revised)

The most committed and fanatical members of the Waffen-SS have been formed into new Shocktrooper units to maximise their impact on the front line. Well equipped, and wearing the latest body armour, they often form the spearhead of assault operations.

Cost	90pts (Regular)
Team	1 NCO and 4 men
Weapons	Assault Rifles
Options	- Add up to 5 additional men with assault rifles for +18pts each. - 1 squad per platoon may be upgraded to Veteran at +2pts per model. - Up to 2 men can have an LMG for +10pts each, for each LMG added another man becomes its loader. - Up to 4 men can have a panzerfaust in addition to other weapons for +5pts each. - Up to 2 men can have rifle grenades for +20pts each.
Special Rules	- Tough - Fanatic - IR Vision

ANTI-TANK GUNS
Towed Schwerefeld Projektor

Improvements in Rift-tech power sources have enabled the scientific minds in Dresden to gradually reduce the size of the earliest Rift-tech weaponry. One such system is the Towed Schwerefeld Projektor, the placing of a projector weapon system onto a towed artillery mount with a separate power unit also towed by the same vehicle. Entrusted to, and crewed by, the new elite Heavy Armoured Infantry, it has replaced some PaK 40 guns in many Heavy Infantry units as it is lighter and easier to manoeuvre.

Cost	120pts (Veteran)
Team	3 men
Weapons	Schwerefeld Projektor
Special Rules	- Team Weapon - Fixed - Resilient - Large Infantry - Towed as a medium gun

German Falschimjäger infantry

ARMOURED CARS
SdKfz 234/X Puma

The SdKfz 234 series of eight-wheeled armoured cars provided a heavy enough platform to trial a lighter version of the Schwerefeld Projektor. The chassis had already proven itself capable of mounting heavier weapons, and the speed and manoeuvrability of the vehicle makes it a formidable tank hunter when armed with Rift-tech weaponry. With this turret, the SdKfz 234/X is not normally employed in the reconnaissance role and its crews are trained to outmanoeuvre heavier armoured targets and disrupt their ability to move freely, leaving them vulnerable to anti-tank guns or heavier tanks.

Cost	145pts (Regular), 160pts (Veteran)
Weapons	1 turret-mounted light Schwerefeld Projektor
Damage Value	7+ (armoured car)
Special Rules	- Front and rear drive (may reverse at Run movement rate)

SdKfz 250/3, 250/5 and 251/6 Armoured Command Half-Tracks

These variants of the 250 series half-track armoured personnel carriers were equipped with additional radios and even map tables and enciphering equipment, turning them into reasonably advanced mobile command posts.

Cost	72pts (Inexperienced), 90pts (Regular), 108pts (Veteran)
Weapons	1 pintle-mounted forward-facing MMG
Damage Value	7+ (armoured carrier)
Special Rules	- Open-topped - Command Vehicle

ARMOURED RECOVERY VEHICLES
Bergepanther

Built on the now reliable Panther chassis, the Bergepanther is able to recover all but the heaviest of fighting vehicles. Highly skilled crews are specifically trained to recover Rift-tech weaponry from the battlefield to prevent it falling into enemy hands.

Cost	102pts (Inexperienced), 128pts (Regular), 154pts (Veteran)
Weapons	1 pintle-mounted forward-facing MMG
Damage Value	9+ (medium tank)
Options	- May replace MMG with forward-facing 20mm light automatic cannon for +20pts.
Special Rules	- ARV - Open-topped - Heavy Front Armour (Damage value is 10+ in the front arc)

Tank Recovery Tractor

All nations use variations of the humble tractor to recover damaged combat vehicles. The variety is endless, from commandeered agricultural machines to military models with lightly armoured cabs and weaponry for self-defence.

Cost	10pts (Inexperienced), 12pts (Regular), 14pts (Veteran)
Weapons	None
Damage Value	6+ (soft-skin)
Options	- May add a pintle-mounted forward-facing MMG for +15pts.
Special Rules	- ARV

THE UNITED STATES

These additional units may be fielded in an American force in line with the normal force selection rules. America's industrial might and steady development of Rift-tech weapons gives confidence to the Allied leadership, but the need to defeat an apparently resurgent Germany and resilient Japan weighs heavy on the President.

HEADQUARTERS UNITS
Armoured Officer

The US have poured substantial resources in to their Armoured Infantry programme, creating entire battalions of armoured companies, and they are now producing specialist armour with enhanced radios for its commanders. Any platoon that contains at least two Armoured Infantry squads may be led by an Armoured Officer instead of the normal officer HQ selection.

Cost	- Second Lieutenant 80pts (Veteran) - First Lieutenant 105pts (Veteran) - Captain 140pts (Veteran) - Major 180pts (Veteran)
Team	1 officer and up to 2 further men
Weapons	SMG (officer), assault rifles (men)
Options	- The officer may be accompanied by up to 2 men at a cost of +21pts per man (Veteran).
Special Rules	- Resilient - Large Infantry - IR Vision - Must have two Heavy Armoured Infantry squads in the platoon to field this unit.

Paragon Officer Slammer Samuels

Captain Harris 'Slammer' Samuels volunteered for the US Paragon programme after earning the Silver Star as a young officer in Tunisia. A natural leader and gifted tactician, Samuels was an obvious choice for the Paragon programme and passed all the entry tests easily. The programme's genetic enhancement worked flawlessly and Samuels quickly mastered the Rift-tech weaponry provided to him, so much so that he has been issued an experimental heavy Tesla rifle that is not yet in service with the rest of the programme. Samuels is an inspiring giant of a man, leading from the front and getting those around him to live up to standards he sets.

Cost	155pts (Veteran)
Team	1 officer
Weapons	Heavy Tesla rifle, Tesla Gauntlet
Special Rules	- Captain (has all normal Officer rules) - Fast - Tough - Tough Fighter - Tank Hunter - Get Moving (when Samuels is activated, all friendly infantry and artillery units within 6" can immediately remove one pin marker)

TESLA GAUNTLET

The Tesla Gauntlet issued to Samuels combines a pneumatic punch with an electrical discharge. In hand-to-hand combat, Samuels gains a +1 modifier to any damage rolls against infantry or artillery targets. Against vehicles it counts as an anti-tank weapon, giving him the Tank Hunter special rule.

US Heavy Bazooka Team

Slammer Samuels

INFANTRY SQUADS
Paragon Squad

The US Paragon programme is a highly secret application of Rift-tech science that looks to enhance human genetics and biology at a molecular level. Results have been highly variable but the success rate is considered worthy of continuing the programme. Whilst few candidates have responded as well as Captain Samuels, several of the Paragons display abilities almost as strong.

When selecting a Paragon squad, choose three of the six Paragons below, each Paragon has a unique skill that only that model can use, and adds a skill to the whole squad.

Cost	70pts (Veteran)
Team	3 Paragons
Weapons	See below
Options	- Select three of the following Paragon troopers (note that if no NCO is selected, then the squad's base Morale is only 9). Each model has unique skills applicable to itself and adds skills to the whole unit while it is alive.
Special Rules	- Fast - Tough - Immune to Horror (do not suffer any penalties caused by Horror)

Paragon Trooper	'Grease'	Max 'The Hatchet' Ashby	John 'Sue' Walton	Sadao Munemori	Cpl Zigmont 'The Monster' Macrathus	Sgt Abraham 'Hammer' Marshall
Weapons	Shotgun	Axe and SMG	2 SMGs	Sword	BAR	Heavy Tesla Rifle
Model Skills	- Strong	- Tooth & Claw	- May fire both SMGs at same time	- Tooth & Claw	- NCO - Tooth & Claw - Strong	- NCO - Strong
Unit Skills	- Tank Hunter	- Tough Fighter	- Vehicle Skill: Agile (applies to any transport used by the squad)	- Fanatic	- Stubborn	- Stubborn

ANTI-TANK GUNS
Tesla AT Gun

The Tesla cannon being deployed on a Sherman chassis, research continued into miniaturising and enhancing he clearly potent technology –in particular the size of the power packs needed to generate sufficient charge. Infantry versions were workable for far lower power weapons, but a breakthrough in January 197 resulted in the first practical trials of lighter, towed weapon systems. By June 1947, a towed Tesla anti-tank gun was deployed in combat. The bulk of these weapons have been deployed to Armoured infantry formations.

Cost	115pts (Veteran)
Team	3 men
Weapons	M17 Tesla cannon
Special Rules	- Team Weapon - Fixed - Resilient - Large Infantry - IR Vision - Towed as a medium gun

US M5A6 Jackal light Walker

Jump to it - US Fireflies and a Mudskipper walker

WALKERS

M3A2 Pondskater Scout Walker

Having suffered at the hands of German and Soviet recce walkers, the US looked to develop a lightweight scout walker that could operate in highly difficult terrain and provide a recce vehicle more versatile than the reliable M8 armoured car. The M3A2 Pondskater was originally conceived by the US Marine Corps but was quickly brought into Army service once it had passed initial field trials. Light enough to be carried by glider, and small enough to deploy from an infantry landing craft, the Pondskater acts as a recce vehicle in the US Army, but also as an infantry weapons platform in the USMC, mounting a M20 Recoilless Rifle or twin .50 cal HMGs.

Cost	75pts (Regular), 95pts (Veteran)
Weapons	360-degree pintle-mounted HMG, forward-mounted hull MMG.
Damage Value	6+ (scout walker)
Options	- May add a second HMG on the pintle mount for +25pts. - May replace any or all HMGs with a single forward-mounted light anti-tank gun for +30pts.
Special Rules	- Recce (if armed with single HMG) - Open-topped - Fast - Agile - Walker - HE – instead of causing HE(D2) hits, a HE shell causes HE(D3) hits. AT gun

M2 Mudskipper Jump Walker (Revised)

The Mudskipper is one of the newest walkers off the production line, a heavier platform to give the Jump Infantry some genuine punch as they advance into enemy territory. With shock absorbers to handle the jumping manoeuvre and a stripped down chassis to save weight, the Mudskipper is proving a battle-winning addition to Jump battalions. The M2A1 variant replaces the arm-mounted .50 cals with anti-tank rockets for additional firepower.

Cost	240pts (Veteran)
Weapons	2 forward-facing, linked casement mounted light autocannons with co-axial MMG. 2 HMGs (1 left arm, 1 right arm). Two Fists.
Damage Value	8+ (medium walker)
Options	- May replace HMGs with arm-mounted bazookas for +10pts per arm.
Special Rules	- Walker - Jump - Assault - Fist

M8 Grizzly ARV

The versatility of the Grizzly chassis saw it utilised for many tasks, including that of a highly mobile ARV. Replacing a fist for a utility lifter and engineering arm, a crane assembly was added to the hull. Reliable and able to get to damaged vehicles in difficult terrain, its arms and crane combination could often lift lighter vehicles out of trouble. It is highly popular with its crew, as the vehicle can complete many tasks without them having to dismount. Some ARVs were seconded to engineer units to assist with route clearance and obstacle clearing and creation.

Cost	115pts (Regular), 132pts (Veteran)
Weapons	1 pintle-mounted HMG, 1 Fist
Damage Value	8+ (medium walker)
Special Rules	- Walker - ARV - Assault - Fist

ARMOURED CARS

M8A3 Tesla Scout

When the Rift-tech programme offered the US Army a smaller version of the Tesla cannon, the immediate solution was fit the weapon onto both the M5 Stuart and M8 Greyhound for trials. Both versions proved viable and the decision was made to put the M8 variant into production first for trials with reconnaissance units and to consider the need for a light tank variant at a later date, either on the M5 Stuart or M24 Chaffee chassis. The addition of the Tesla cannon on the M8 gave recce units more versatility against infantry whilst maintaining anti-tank capability against their German counterparts such as the Spinne and Puma. The lack of recoil in the Tesla system meant very little work was needed on the chassis, although the weight of the batteries has shortened the lifespan of the vehicle's suspension and gearbox, a worthwhile sacrifice from the crew's perspective.

Cost	118pts (Regular), 145pts (Veteran)
Weapons	1 turret-mounted M21 light Tesla cannon
Damage Value	7+ (armoured car)
Options	- May add pintle-mounted HMG with 360-degree arc of fire for +25pts.
Special Rules	- Recce

ARMOURED RECOVERY VEHICLES

M32 ARV

Built on the now ubiquitous Sherman chassis, the M32 ARV is mobile and well equipped, but lacks some of the pulling power now required to assist the heavy fighting vehicles present on the battlefield. What it lacks in strength it often makes up for in numbers.

Cost	77pts (Inexperienced), 96pts (Regular), 115pts (Veteran)
Weapons	1 forward-facing hull-mounted MMG
Damage Value	9+ (medium tank)
Special Rules	- ARV

Tank Recovery Tractor

All nations use variations of the humble tractor to recover damaged combat vehicles. The variety is endless, from commandeered agricultural machines to military models with lightly armoured cabs and weaponry for self-defence

Cost	10pts (Inexperienced), 12pts (Regular), 14pts (Veteran)
Weapons	None
Damage Value	6+ (soft-skin)
Options	- May add a pintle-mounted forward-facing MMG for +15pts.
Special Rules	- ARV

GREAT BRITAIN AND THE COMMONWEALTH

This list provides additional units that can be included in any Great Britain and Commonwealth force selection. The Commonwealth continues to fight all over the globe, from Europe to the Far East. Only Germany's defeat will now satisfy the weary British population.

HEADQUARTERS UNITS
Galahad Armoured Infantry Officer

As the numbers of units equipped with the Rift-tech designed Galahad armour increases, the creation of fully equipped infantry battalions is now feasible and platoon, company and even battalion HQs are now entering the field in Galahad armour.

Cost	- Second Lieutenant 85pts (Veteran) - First Lieutenant 110pts (Veteran) - Captain 145pts (Veteran) - Major 185pts (Veteran)
Team	1 officer and up to 1 further man
Weapons	Officer SMG, man LMG
Options	- The officer may be accompanied by 1 man at a cost of +35pts (Veteran).
Special Rules	- Large Infantry - Resilient - Tough - Slow

INFANTRY SQUADS
War Dog Squad

Whilst the average Tommy is reluctant to tackle some of the horrors of the modern battlefield, specially trained and bred war dogs have few problems in doing so. With the increasing influence of Rift-tech science to make the dogs faster and stronger, packs of these animals can be released to savage the enemy. The handlers of these dogs are usually quite relieved when they can retire to the rear having set the dogs on their course of destruction.

Cost	31pts (Regular)
Team	1 NCO and 3 war dogs
Weapons	Pistol (NCO handler only)
Options	- Add up to 2 additional handlers with Pistols for +10pts (Regular) each. - Add up to 6 additional war dogs +7pts (regular)
Special Rules	- War Dog

British Armoured Infantry

The British catch a German column unaware

British Armoured Infantry

Grenadier Section

In order to test new equipment and technology coming from the UK's Rift-tech labs and workshops, the 7th Bn Grenadier Guards were seconded to the Rift Research Department in order to provide troops to trial new equipment and technology. Once initial trials were completed, platoons of the Battalion would deploy forward to test the equipment on the front line, often to the benefit of the infantry they were supporting, but occasionally proving a project a disappointing failure. Over the past two years, the Battalion has developed a greater understanding of the weaponry at its disposal and is now considered an elite shock unit as much as an R&D unit. This of course fits nicely with the role the Grenadiers and the Guards Division has played in the British Army's history. Although technically still part of the Guard's Division, the unit is often referred to as The Grenadiers, or more recently, the Rift Grenadiers.

Cost	60pts (Regular), 75pts (Veteran)
Team	1 NCO and 4 men
Weapons	Rifles
Options	- Add up to 5 additional men with rifles for +12pts (Regular) or +15pts (Veteran) each. - Any model can replace their rifle with an assault rifle for +5pts each - Up to 2 men can replace their rifle with a heavy Tesla rifle for +15pts, one other man becomes a loader for each Tesla rifle taken. - Up to 3 men can have rifle grenades for +15pts each. - The entire squad may be given anti-tank grenades at +2pts per man.
Special Rules	- Tank Hunters (if grenades taken) - Stubborn - IR Vision

ANTI-TANK GUNS
Tesla AT Gun

With the introduction of towed Tesla weapons within US Armoured Infantry units, the British government demanded immediate access to the designs. Conscious of the lack of anti-tank firepower in the small, elite Galahad battalions, the Tesla AT gun was a natural solution. The US promptly provided the necessary designs but are unable to ship significant numbers of weapons across the Atlantic; within Great Britain, production speeds are proving slower than originally hoped but Galahad formations are beginning to receive these support systems.

Cost	120pts (Veteran)
Team	3 men
Weapons	M17 Tesla cannon
Special Rules	- Team Weapon - Fixed - Resilient - Tough - IR Vision - Large Infantry - towed as medium gun

TANKS
Churchill Meteor

The large size and suspension of the Churchill tank makes it an ideal hull on which to test experimental weapons. The Meteor Turret is a variation of the US Calliope, carrying Rift-tech designed rockets containing a metal-weakening enzyme as well as explosive ordinance. The Churchill retains its normal weaponry but may launch a Meteor rocket barrage instead of firing its main weapon. The weight of the weapon system hardly impacts the performance of the Churchill, and the tanks survivability means it can normally get into position to launch its rockets to best effect.

Cost	340pts (Regular), 410pts (Veteran)
Weapons	1 turret-mounted medium anti-tank gun with co-axial MMG. 1 turret mounted Meteor rocket launcher. 1 forward-facing hull-mounted MMG.
Damage Value	10+ (heavy tank)
Special Rules	- Slow - HE – instead of causing HE(D2) hits, a HE shell causes HE(D6) hits. - May not fire Meteor launcher and AT gun in the same turn.

WALKERS
Automated Mobile Platform

Having succeeded in automating an armoured carrier, the British Rift-tech Division looked to develop the concept further, combining the continuing improvements in AI technology with a purpose built chassis capable of carrying several weapon systems in a universal mount. This would allow rapid changes in weapon load to suit specific missions. Originally conceived as a walker with legs, Rift-tech advances, and an experimental track design have resulted in a highly agile tracked chassis that gives more stable, but comparable manoeuvrability. After successful trials, the Automated Mobile Platform or AMP was declared combat ready and three weapon loads were finalised. The Hunter mounts an anti-tank gun, the Bombardier carries a light howitzer, whilst the Lancer mounts an anti-aircraft HMG system. The AMP's design allows it to manoeuvre its gun shield to better protect itself from fire, particularly when stationary or when attacked from the flanks. As the AMP usually operates in packs, up to two AMPs can be selected as a single light walker selection.

Cost	95pts (Regular)
Weapons	1 forward facing hull-mounted medium anti-tank gun. 2 fists
Damage Value	6+ (scout walker)
Options	- Bombardier, may replace anti-tank gun with light howitzer for -15pts. - Lancer, may replace anti-tank gun with three linked HMGs for +5pts.
Special Rules	- Walker - Automaton - Fist - Assault - Agile - Tough (against attacks hitting the walker's front arc) - Flak (when armed with HMGs)

British heavy infantry supported by automatons

M5A5/6 Jackal Light Walker

British airborne forces now employ limited numbers of Jackal walkers to support glider and parachute infantry. Despite US reluctance to deliver the Jackal in large quantities, it is hugely popular with the infantry it supports and its success is the driving force behind plans for the creation of British Airborne Jump Infantry formations.

Cost	90pts (Regular), 105pts (Veteran)
Weapons	Right arm mounted MMG and 2 Fists
Damage Value	7+ (light walker)
Options	- May add infantry flamethrower to left arm for +20pts.
Special Rules	- Walker - Agile - Assault - Fist - Jump - Single Crew (may only fire one weapon each turn)

Grizzly Medium Assault Walker (Revised)

Provided under the combination of lend-lease financing and in exchange for British engineering knowledge, the Grizzly is the watchword for rugged and practical. Armed with the proven 75mm gun and a .50 HMG, the Grizzly is versatile and adaptable. Perhaps even more useful are the powerful arms that can smash tanks and clear obstacles. Well liked by its crews, the Grizzly is considered a better infantry support option than the Sherman, particularly in urban environments where it can carry out improvised route clearance and help build defensive obstacles.

Cost	200pts (Regular), 245pts (Veteran)
Weapons	1 forward-facing casement-mounted medium anti-tank gun. Pintle-mounted HMG. 2 Fists.
Damage Value	8+ (medium walker)
Special Rules	- Walker - Assault - Fist - HE – instead of causing HE(D2) hits, a HE shell causes HE(D6) hits.

M2 Mudskipper

The success of the US Mudskipper with their airborne forces prompted the British to consider similar jump formations. Whilst the development of Jump Infantry is not yet complete, the introduction of limited numbers of Mudskipper and Jackal walkers into the British Airborne Division has been carried out on a trial basis. US hesitancy to share the jump technology has

been overcome through persistence and the logic of enhancing British airborne forces to share the load on future Allied operations.

Cost	240pts (Veteran)
Weapons	2 forward-facing, linked casement mounted light autocannons with co-axial MMG. 2 HMG (1 left arm, 1 right arm). 2 Fists.
Damage Value	8+ (medium walker)
Options	- May replace HMGs with arm-mounted bazookas for +10pts per arm.
Special Rules	- Walker - Jump - Assault - Fist

Hornet Medium Walker

Whilst the effectiveness of the US Kodiak in both an anti-aircraft and anti-materiel role was clearly apparent, British procurement officers were concerned at the ammunition and logistical demands the walker presented. It was also believed that the lack of utility arms would be detrimental to the walker as it navigated urban and rough terrain. This led to the US offers of the US Kodiak in the Lend Lease programme being refused. Instead, the British developed the Hornet based on the Grizzly chassis' they had already received. The Hornet had a reduced anti-aircraft field of fire, but was primarily designed to support infantry in close, urban terrain. Its utility arms can clear obstacles, build improvised defences and rip apart light vehicles, whilst its array of quad-HMGs and a short-barrelled, heavy automatic cannon is more than capable of suppressing dug in infantry and vehicles within close terrain. Whilst it has no anti-tank capability beyond arm's reach, a platoon of Hornets would normally include a standard Grizzly as a 'gun walker' to provide some anti-tank protection.

Cost	210pts (Regular), 255pts (Veteran)
Weapons	1 forward facing casement-mounted heavy automatic cannon. 4 linked, forward facing, casement-mounted HMGs. 2 Fists
Damage Value	8+ (medium walker)
Special Rules	- Walker - Assault - Flak (front arc only) - Fist - Short Barrel (heavy automatic cannon range reduced to 48")

ARMOURED RECOVERY VEHICLES

Churchill ARV

The massive Churchill tank is slow but incredibly powerful, making it an excellent platform to base an ARV upon.

Cost	122pts (Inexperienced), 152pts (Regular), 182pts (Veteran)
Weapons	1 forward-facing hull-mounted MMG
Damage Value	10+ (heavy tank)
Special Rules	- ARV - Slow

Cromwell ARV

Although supplied with large numbers of the US M32 Sherman ARVs, the British prefer the slightly more mobile Cromwell chassis, particularly when supporting Cromwell-equipped formations.

Cost	77pts (Inexperienced), 96pts (Regular), 115pts (Veteran)
Weapons	1 forward-facing hull-mounted MMG
Damage Value	9+ (medium tank)
Special Rules	- ARV

Tank Recovery Tractor

All nations use variations of the humble tractor to recover damaged combat vehicles. The variety is endless, from commandeered agricultural machines to military models with lightly armoured cabs and weaponry for self-defence.

Cost	10pts (Inexperienced), 12pts (Regular), 14pts (Veteran)
Weapons	None
Damage Value	6+ (soft-skin)
Options	- May add a pintle-mounted forward-facing MMG for +15pts.
Special Rules	- ARV

Daughters of the Motherland on the move

SOVIET UNION

This list provides additional units that can be included in any Soviet Union force selection. The Soviet juggernaut moves relentlessly west but the morale of the average fighting soldier remains less than it should. By fielding the products of Soviet Rift-tech, the enemies of the Motherland shall be defeated.

HEADQUARTERS UNITS

Commissar Gregor Drugov

Commissar Drugov was always a large, brutal bully of a man who found a natural home in the Soviet Political Commissariat where his fervour and brutal nature gained him rapid recognition and promotion. As the Soviets perfected the use of their stolen Rift-tech, trusted volunteers were sought to trial the initial genetic manipulation programmes. Drugov volunteered for an advanced version of the Ursine Programme and received a carefully modified treatment that delivered the physical benefits of the ursine whilst reducing the bestial side effects. Not that Drugov is any less bestial than he was prior to the treatment! As a commissar he stalks the front lines, driving the soldiers in front of him forward relentlessly and with the zeal of a natural bully. His actions are encouraged by his superiors, who recognise the fragile morale of the Soviet Army. To assist Drugov in his task he has been assigned two bodyguards in the form of veteran Ursus troopers who use their bulk to protect Drugov from harm.

Soviet Daughters of the Motherland

Cost	105pts (Veteran)
Team	Commissar Drugov and 2 Ursus soldiers
Weapons	Assault rifle (Drugov only)
Options	- Drugov may be accompanied by 1 man at a cost of +35pts (Veteran).
Special Rules	- Large Infantry (Ursus only) - Resilient - Tough (Ursus only) * The owning player allocates all damage to the Ursus bodyguards until they are dead, then allocates remaining damage to Drugov. Exceptional damage results can be allocated directly to Drugov. - Horror - Tooth and Claw - Strong - Not One Step Back (Drugov only) - Motivate (Drugov only; when using Motivate, remove a model from the target unit as per the Not One Step Back rule)

Daughters of the Motherland Patriot Team

The Daughters of the Motherland have become a regular sight on Soviet news reels and often feature on radio broadcasts. To maximise their media profile, a plan was developed to increase their presence on the battlefield and thereby bolster the (often low) morale of the average Soviet infantryman. Pairs of Daughters are attached to regular infantry platoons to provide a patriotic focal point for the fighting soldiers. To further encourage their acceptance amongst the common soldier, they carry both assault rifles and a new Soviet Rift-tech sonic shield generator that can deflect and disrupt incoming fire.

Cost	65pts when added to Regular squad, 70pts when added to Veteran squad
Team	2 Daughters of the Motherland (Veteran)
Weapons	Assault rifle and Shield Proyektor

Special Rules	- Fast
	- Grants the unit the following special rules until both Daughters are killed:
	  - Stubborn
	  - Tough
	- May be added to any non-Resilient, Regular or Veteran infantry officer or Infantry squad (not weapon teams)

A Soviet IS-3 heavy Tank

INFANTRY SQUADS

Heavy Infantry Squad (Revised)

The German version appeared on the battlefield first, and the US were not far behind with their Heavy Armoured Infantry. In a rush to keep up with their foes, Soviet armour was developed quickly and put into use not long after their rivals. Cumbersome and bulky, the Soviet suits lack subtlety, but their effectiveness is not disputed. Unlike other nations, the Soviet Heavy Infantry was considered more of an anti-vehicle unit.

Cost	140pts (Veteran)
Team	1 NCO and 4 men
Weapons	Dual weapon pack
Options	- Add up to 5 additional men with dual weapon packs for +28pts each. - Up to 4 men can add a second dual weapon pack for +20pts each, these models can fire both packs when shooting.
Special Rules	- Resilient - Large Infantry - Slow - Tank Hunter - Dual Weapon System (select 1 mode when firing, AT rifle suffers no PEN reduction at long range)

DUAL WEAPON PACK				
Type	Range (")	Shots	PEN	Special Rules
AT Rifle	18	1	+2	
SMG	6	2	-	Assault

TANKS

IS-3 Heavy Tank

The IS-3 is a major redesign of the earlier IS-2, retaining the powerful 122mm gun but housed in a new dome-shaped turret. Its sharply sloped front armour provides incredible protection with a low silhouette. First entering service in 1946, the IS-3 has been given to several Guards Tank Regiments to take the fight to the Germans.

Cost	480pts (Inexperienced), 600pts (Regular), 720pts (Veteran)
Weapons	1 turret-mounted heavy anti-tank gun with co-axial MMG, 1 pintle-mounted HMG on turret
Damage Value	11+ (super-heavy tank)
Special Rules	- HE – instead of causing D3 HE hits, an HE shell causes 2D6 hits. - Advanced Armour (Damage value of 12+ against shots hitting its front armour)

WALKERS

Mastadon Heavy Walker

The successful impact of the Mammoth on the battlefield gave the Soviet engineers the opportunity to develop the chassis further. Impressed by the impact the Zeus had made on battlefields across Europe, the Soviets attempted to replicate the vehicle on the Mammoth chassis. Using the heaviest 122mm gun available, the Mastadon could not quite replicate the anti-tank capability of the Zeus, but retained a useful HE capability due to the size of the 122mm shell.

Cost	320pts (Regular), 385pts (Veteran)
Weapons	1 turret-mounted heavy anti-tank gun with co-axial MMG, and 1 forward-facing hull-mounted MMG
Damage Value	10+ (super-heavy walker)
Options	- May add dozer blade for +25pts
Special Rules	- Walker - Tough (from front arc only if dozer blade fitted) - Slow - HE – instead of causing HE(D3) hits, a HE shell causes HE(2D6) hits.

ARMOURED RECOVERY VEHICLES

T-34 ARV

As the Soviet Union moves to ever heavier and larger tanks in the front line, the volume of damaged and repaired T-34s is staggering. Many of these are being converted into ARV vehicles to keep the heavier tanks and walkers in the fight. Their speed and mobility also makes them capable of targeting disabled enemy Rift-tech machines for capture and exploitation.

Cost	77pts (Inexperienced), 96pts (Regular), 115pts (Veteran)
Weapons	1 forward-facing hull-mounted MMG
Damage Value	9+ (medium tank)
Special Rules	- ARV

TANK RECOVERY TRACTOR

All nations use variations of the humble tractor to recover damaged combat vehicles. The variety is endless, from commandeered agricultural machines to military models with lightly armoured cabs and weaponry for self-defence.

Cost	10pts (Inexperienced), 12pts (Regular), 14pts (Veteran)
Weapons	None
Damage Value	6+ (soft-skin)
Options	- May add a pintle-mounted forward-facing MMG for +15pts.
Special Rules	- ARV

Soviet T-34 ZP

JAPANESE AND FINNISH ARMY LISTS

The following pages introduce two new forces in to the *Konflikt '47* world: the swift and ferocious Imperial Japanese Army and the stalwart and hardy Finnish Resistance Forces. The Japanese have perhaps achieved the greatest grasp of the new Rift-technology and have made significant advances using German research as a starting point. Meanwhile, the embattled nation of Finland is under Soviet control, but Finnish Resistance and German-backed forces engage the occupiers with a resource-draining campaign of attrition.

JAPAN

This list is based upon the troops and equipment available to the Imperial Japanese Army and Navy forces in this latter period of the war in Asia and the Pacific. The Japanese Army began the war using infantry equipped with bolt-action rifles, light machine guns, grenades and all the paraphernalia of modern warfare. By 1945, they had recognised the need to modernise their forces, and to conserve their resources for a lengthy struggle. The delivery of Rift-tech from Germany provided Japanese scientists with several unique opportunities to advance the Imperial cause and by 1947 the Japanese Army possessed some of the most advanced weaponry of the conflict. When combined with the natural tenacity of the Japanese soldier, the combination is a menacing threat to their enemies.

ARMY SPECIAL RULES
Death Before Dishonour
Many Japanese soldiers and officers believe that a display of will through personal sacrifice will win the war for Japan. An appropriate offer in blood would at least ensure a spiritual victory.

Every unit in this list has the Fanatics special rule, as described on page 30 of this book.

Banzai Charge
Japanese forces often use massed, frenzied charges often with the cry 'Banzai!' These charges are sometimes effective, but is more often are simply a waste of good men. If a Japanese infantry unit is ordered to Run towards (or charge) the closest visible enemy, any order test for that move is automatically passed, as if the unit had rolled a double one. All models in the unit must then make a full move directly towards one of the models in the target unit, and must make contact with the target unit if possible. Note that a unit can be ordered to Run/charge in another direction, but in that case it will follow the normal rules and the Banzai Charge rule has no effect.

SNLF Officer making a banzi charge

Ambush Tactics
Japanese infantrymen are masters at using cover to set ambushes and spring surprise attacks on the enemy. Also, it has become all too apparent to the Japanese that their tanks are generally no match for the Allied tanks and walkers that oppose them. The only recourse is to attempt to conceal tanks amongst undergrowth or in other cover, and ambush enemy vehicles.

During set-up, any Japanese unit starting the game Hidden (as described on page 120 of the *Konflikt '47* rulebook) may start the game already in Ambush. If you decide to do so, set one of your order dice in place next to them, as if you had ordered them to Ambush.

Show Your Loyalty!
Imperial Japanese platoons can include Kempeitai political officers. Kempeitai officers don't confer any morale bonus to nearby troops like other officers. However, the presence of these feared officers is useful in steeling the nerve of untried units, such as militia. If a Green friendly Japanese unit within 6" of the Kempeitai officer rolls for its Green special rule, the player may re-roll the result.

TYPES OF UNIT

1	Infantry	Headquarters units
		Infantry squads
		Infantry teams
2	Artillery	Anti-tank guns
		Field artillery
3	Vehicles	Tanks
		Tank destroyers
		Walkers
		Armoured cars
		Tankettes
		Self-propelled artillery
		Anti-aircraft vehicles
		Transports and tows

US Marines try to halt a Gaikokkaku beach landing

HEADQUARTERS UNITS

Each platoon is centred upon a core that includes a headquarters unit in the form of a First or Second Lieutenant. Other HQ units can be added to the force, including higher-ranking officers, as well as medical units and supporting observers.

Kempeitai Political Officer

A much-feared political police force, the Kempeitai are heavily involved with the training and indoctrination of militia and colonial units. Their brutal and often cruel methods, together with the brainwashing effect of their propaganda, ensures that even poorly armed and barely trained civilians of occupied territories are a threat to potential aggressors.

Cost	15pts (Inexperienced)
Team	1 Kempeitai political officer and up to 2 further men
Weapons	Pistol, SMG, rifle or as depicted on the models
Options	- The political officer may be accompanied by up to 2 men at a cost of +7pts (Inexperienced) per man.
Special Rules	- Show Your Loyalty!

Kempeitai Officer

Officer

Imperial Japanese officers are capable and often experienced leaders that can have a very dramatic effect on their soldiers. An officer unit consists of the man himself and can include up to two other soldiers acting as his immediate attendants. Because of the high quality of the majority of Japanese officers, we rate them as Regular or Veteran. Most officers use the 8mm Type 14 pistol – an improved model of the Nambu pistol.

Cost	- Second Lieutenant (Rikugun Shoi) 50pts (Regular), 65 pts (Veteran) - First Lieutenant (Rikugun Chui) 75pts (Regular), 90pts (Veteran) - Captain (Rikugun Taii) 110pts (Regular), 125pts (Veteran) - Major (Rikugun Shosa) 150pts (Regular), 165pts (Veteran)
Team	1 officer and up to 2 further men
Weapons	Pistol, sword, SMG, rifle or assault rifle as depicted on the model
Options	- The officer may be accompanied by up to 2 men at a cost of +10pts per man (Regular) or +13pts per man (Veteran).
Special Rules	- Tough Fighter (officer only, must have sword)

Medic

The field medic presents the wounded soldier with his best chance of surviving serious injury and can ensure that lightly wounded soldiers are returned to fighting fitness as rapidly as possible. Junior medical staff such as stretcher-bearers can accompany medics in the field. As non-combatants, medics do not often carry weapons – but the practicalities of war sometimes led to medical staff carrying pistols for their personal protection. We rate them as Regular or Veteran.

Cost	Medic 23pts (Regular), 30pts (Veteran)
Team	1 Medic and up to 2 further men
Weapons	Pistol or none as depicted on the model
Options	- The medic may be accompanied by up to 2 men at a cost of +10pts per man (Regular) or +13pts per man (Veteran).

Forward Observer

Forward observers are liaison officers responsible for co-ordinating the attack of heavy artillery batteries from behind the lines or aircraft strikes. They are likely to be accompanied by a radio operator and other immediate attendants. We rate these officers as Regular or Veteran, those of lesser ability being unlikely to find themselves in such an important position.

Cost	- Artillery Forward Observer 100pts (Regular), 115pts (Veteran) - Air Force Forward Observer 75pts (Regular), 90pts (Veteran)
Team	1 Forward Observer and up to 2 further men
Weapons	Pistol, SMG, rifle as depicted on the model
Options	- The observer may be accompanied by up to 2 men at a cost of +10pts per man (Regular) or +13pts per man (Veteran).

JAPANESE INFANTRY FORMATIONS

The Allies consider Japanese formations to be of three basic categories: Types A, B and C.

Type A is the army in China and Manchuria. Type B is the army of the Far East and Pacific.

Type C refers to garrison divisions stationed in China and the militias used to pacify occupied territories.

Each type has different levels of supporting arms. Provisions for fielding the differing formations are made within the lists where appropriate.

INFANTRY SQUADS & TEAMS

During the early phases of the Pacific War, the Japanese soldier excelled against his enemies. He quickly adapted to jungle fighting that was very different from the kind of warfare he was used to in China and Manchuria. He was supported by a technically advanced air force and transported across the sea by a powerful and modern navy.

As the reach of the Japanese Empire grew, so did the strain on the logistics needed to maintain the military on the front foot. The Army was rescued from this over-extension by the Imperial Navy and its new Rift-tech stealth submarines that forced the Allied navies away from the vital sea lanes that Japan relied upon. The arrival of Rift-tech battle-frames further extended the power and reach of the IJA. The Japanese infantryman remains a highly motivated and capable combatant, willing to die before surrendering, but his commanders have begun to learn the value of living to fight another day and increasingly husband their resources whilst expending militia and conscripted soldiers recruited from the occupied territories.

IJA Infantry Squad

The Imperial Japanese Army (IJA) forms the largest component of the Imperial Japanese forces and provides the bulk of the manpower. The 'Type B' IJA infantry squad normally consists of 13 men: an NCO (usually a corporal or Go-Cho) armed with a rifle or a submachine gun, 11 riflemen armed with rifles and a man armed with a Type 96 light machine gun. 'Type A' and 'Type C' squads are larger, including 15 men in total. The introduction of Rift-tech designed compression rifles allows the squad tremendous firepower and has encouraged commanders to engage in longer firefights before resorting to massed charges. The entry below allows you to field either type.

Cost	70 pts (Regular), 91pts (Veteran)
Team	1 NCO and 6 men
Weapons	Rifles
Options	- Add up to 8 additional men with rifles for +10pts (Regular) or +13pts (Veteran) each. - The NCO and up to 1 other man may replace their rifle with an SMG for +3pts each. - Any model may replace their rifle with a compression rifle for +4pts each. - Up to 1 man can have an LMG for +20pts each, another man becomes its loader. - Up to 1 man can have a light mortar for +25pts, another man becomes the loader. - The squad can be given anti-tank grenades for +2pts per model.
Special Rules	- Tank Hunters (if anti-tank grenades taken)

IJA Type Ke-Ho Recce

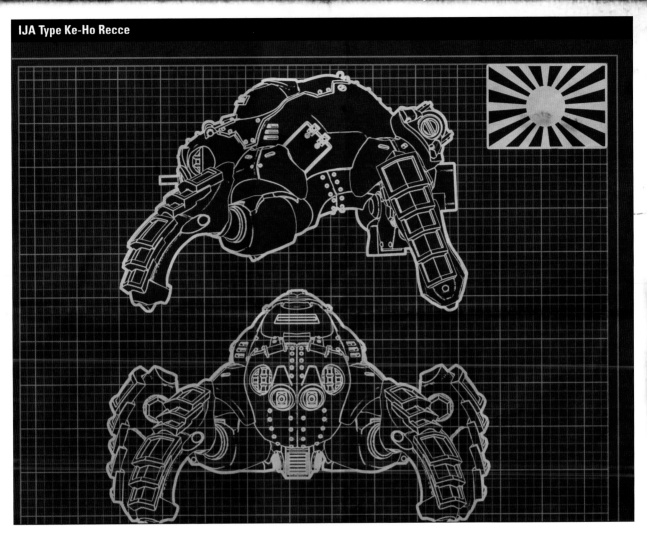

SNLF Squad

The marine troops of the Japanese Navy are known as the Special Naval Landing Force (SNLF) and form part of the Navy Land Forces, founded in the 1930s as a means of providing armed troops that could be landed from ships without having to use armed sailors and thereby reduce a ship's crew. SNLF troops are amongst the best of all Japan's fighting men. They were first deployed in amphibious landings during the war against China, and later during the annexations of overseas Dutch, British and American territories during 1941 and early 1942. Since then, the arm has been used to spearhead numerous landing and assault operations before being replaced by the regular army once they have secured the necessary beachhead.

Cost	65pts (Veteran)
Team	1 NCO and 6 men
Weapons	Rifles
Options	- Add up to 7 additional men with rifles for +13pts (Veteran) each. - The NCO and up to 1 man may replace their rifle with an SMG for +3pts each. - Any model may replace their rifle with a compression rifle for +4pts each. - Up to 1 man can have an LMG for +20pts, another man becomes its loader. - The squad can be given anti-tank grenades for +2pts per model.-
Special Rules	- Tank Hunters (if anti-tank grenades taken)

Special Naval Landing Force

SNLF Grenadier Squad

The SNLF also have Grenadier squads equipped with light but effective mortars to provide fire support to the assaulting infantry sections. Unlike the regular army, these squads remain as dedicated sections and have not had their mortars reallocated within regular SNLF squads.

Cost	65pts (Veteran)
Team	1 NCO and 6 men
Weapons	Rifles
Options	- Add up to 8 additional men with rifles for +13pts (Veteran) each. - The NCO and up to 1 man may replace their rifle with an SMG for +3pts each. - Up to 3 men can have a light mortar for +20pts each, for each mortar added another man becomes its loader. - Up to 1 man can have an LMG for +20pts, another man becomes its loader. - The squad can be given anti-tank grenades for +2pts per model.
Special Rules	-Tank Hunters (if anti-tank grenades taken)

Teishin Shudan Paratrooper Squad

Japanese paratroopers – Teishin Shudan ('raiding group') – proved highly effective in the early years of the war. German successes with paratroops during 1940 encouraged the Japanese to develop their airborne arm as a constituent part of the Imperial Japanese Army Air Force (IJAAF). They were initially deployed in the Dutch East Indies during the Battle of Palambang in February 1942. High casualties amongst the paratroopers discouraged further deployment by air, and the Teishin Shudan subsequently fight as elite infantry formations – much like their German counterparts.

Cost	65pts (Veteran)
Team	1 NCO and 6 men
Weapons	Rifles
Options	- Add up to 5 additional men with rifles for +13pts (Veteran) each. - The NCO and up to 3 men may replace their rifle with an SMG for +3pts each. - Any model may replace their rifle with a compression rifle for +4pts each. - Up to 1 man can have an LMG for +20pts, another man becomes its loader. - The squad can be given anti-tank grenades for +2pts per model.
Special Rules	- Tank Hunters (if anti-tank grenades taken)

A Type 6 Scorpion walker leads Japanese exoskeleton troops into action

Imperial Japanese Army battle exoskeleton squad

Conscript/Militia Squad

In many parts of the recently expanded Japanese Empire, local forces have been raised to supplement the IJA in the garrisoning and security duties of the region. In many cases, these troops find themselves in combat, sometimes willingly, other times not. In the most pro-Japanese areas of Manchuria and China, IJA officers and mentors have led these formations against the Chinese Army with surprising success.

Cost	35pts (Inexperienced)
Team	1 NCO and 4 men
Weapons	Rifles
Options	- Add up to 10 additional men with rifles for +7pts (Inexperienced) each. - The squad can be given anti-tank grenades for +2pts per model.
Special Rules	- Green - Tank Hunters - Not subject to 'Death before Dishonour' national rule

Battle-exoskeleton squad (Sentou-Gaikokkaku Squad)

Granted access to German Rift-tech development, Japanese scientists were able to make significant advances in the new technology, indeed, some of the hints and messages received almost seemed structured to existing Japanese research. One such field was that of exoskeletons, with rapidly led to the armoured battle-frames deployed in mid-1946. These battle-frames enabled soldiers to move freely whilst carrying heavier loads and protective armour. Although the Japanese steered away from fully armoured suits after several fatal trials, the protection afforded by the frames is considerable. The Sentou-Gaikokkaku squads are mobile and carry significant firepower.

Cost	95pts (Veteran)
Team	1 NCO and 4 men
Weapons	SMG
Options	- Add up to 5 additional men with SMGs for +19pts (Veteran) each. - Any model can replace its SMG with a Compression Rifle for +1pts each. - Up to 2 men can replace their SMG with an LMG for +15pts each. - Up to 2 men can add rifle grenades for +20pts each.
Special Rules	- Tough - Fast - IR Vision - Two weapons (rifle grenades can be fired in addition to SMG or compression rifle)

Assault-exoskeleton squad (Totsugeki-Gaikokkaku Squad)

Whilst the battle-frames brought considerable and mobile firepower to support the resolute Japanese infantryman, the need to spearhead assaults against defended position led to variation of the original battle-frame, making it more mobile at the expense of some of squad's heavier firepower. In addition, the Totsugeki-Gaikokkaku troops are extensively trained in using the assault exo-skeleton itself as a weapon in close quarters.

Cost	100pts (Veteran)
Team	1 NCO and 4 men
Weapons	SMG
Options	- Add up to 5 additional men with SMGs +20pts (Veteran) each. - Up to 4 men can replace their SMG with a compression rifle for +13pts.
Special Rules	- Tough - Tough Fighter - Fast - IR Vision

Shibito Squad

Using the Rift-tech technology of the Germans in the animation of recently deceased corpses, the Japanese have managed to advance the process, both in the speed of its application, and the range of subjects that it is applied to. Unlike the German programme, the Japanese have been able to apply the technology to the corpses of Allied soldiers, suggesting a variation in the technology that can override the issues Germany may have faced thus far. The IJA have used these forces to operate on the Pacific islands where their ability to operate without supplies is invaluable.

Cost	64pts (Inexperienced)
Team	8 animated corpses
Weapons	None
Options	- Add up to 16 additional corpses for +8pts each.
Special Rules	- Horror - Slow - Tough - Tough Fighter - Ignore pin markers and morale checks - Not affected by Medics

Ghost Attack Squad (Yurei Kogeki-Tai)

The Japanese Ghost Attack squads are possibly the most feared outputs of the Japanese Rift-tech programme. Finding meaning and understanding in much of the deciphered data provided to them by Germany, the Japanese have made incredible leaps in the science of molecular cohesion. One development of this research is a device that creates a small field capable of phasing out of sync with the material around it. Suitably protected in an extensive protective suit, a wearer can use the field to pass through solid objects, although the short duration of the field, and its occasional failure remains its greatest shortcoming.

Cost	126pts (Veteran)
Team	1 NCO and 6 men
Weapons	Compression rifle
Options	- Any model may replace its compression rifle with an SMG. - May be given anti-tank grenades for +2pts per model
Special Rules	- Tough - Tank Hunter (if grenades taken) - Phase Field – may ignore terrain when moving but not for LOS. When using this ability to ignore terrain, roll a D6 for each model. If any of the D6 rolled comes up a 1, the unit is caught up in the terrain as some phasefields momentarily fail and the unit suffers a pin marker.

Medium Machine Gun Team

The standard Japanese medium machine gun of the war is the 7.7mm calibre Type 1. Introduced in 1941, it is a simplified and lightened version of the Type 92 which also remains in service.

Cost	35pts (Inexperienced), 50pts (Regular), 65pts (Veteran)
Team	3 men
Weapons	1 MMG
Special Rules	- Team Weapon - Fixed

Anti-Tank Rifle Team

The Japanese introduced the Type 97 anti-tank rifle in 1937. It has a calibre of 20mm and is a semi-automatic weapon with a high rate of fire. It is capable of penetrating up to 30mm of armour, sufficient to deal with Heavy Infantry, most lightly armoured vehicles, and even light tanks.

Cost	21pts (Inexperienced), 30pts (Regular), 39pts (Veteran)
Team	2 men
Weapons	1 anti-tank rifle
Special Rules	- Team Weapon

A Japanese medium machine gun team ready for action

Flamethrower Team

Combat engineer units form a constituent part of every IJA division. They carry explosives for demolition work and attacking enemy fortifications, and are also equipped for mine clearance. Some carry the Type 100 flamethrower that saw action in the early years of the War in Indonesia and the Philippines.

Cost	50pts (Regular), 65pts (Veteran)
Team	2 men
Weapons	Infantry flamethrower
Options	- May be given anti-tank grenades for +2pts per model.
Special Rules	- Team Weapon - Flamethrower - Tank Hunter (if grenades taken)

Sniper Team

The jungles of southern Asia provide plenty of opportunity for snipers to make their mark, and the Japanese sniper is well served by the Type 97 sniper rifle with telescopic sight. The rifle is especially suited for use by concealed snipers as its small-calibre bullet and long barrel result in very little muzzle flash or smoke, enabling the shooter to remain unseen by the enemy.

Cost	50pts (Regular), 65pts (Veteran)
Team	2 men
Weapons	1 rifle
Special Rules	- Team Weapon

Light Mortar Team

The Japanese have developed a range of grenades that could, by means of separate adapters, be fired from rifles or the Type 10 and Type 89 grenade launchers. These lightweight weapons are effectively light mortars of 50mm calibre, and the Japanese make great use of them for close-range support. They are mistakenly referred to as 'knee mortars' by the Allies on the erroneous assumption the curved base-plate was braced against the firer's leg. In fact, they are planted firmly on the ground just like other light mortars.

Cost	24pts (Inexperienced), 35pts (Regular), 46pts (Veteran)
Team	2 men
Weapons	1 light mortar
Special Rules	- Team Weapon - Indirect Fire - HE(D3)

Medium Mortar Team

The standard medium mortar of the Japanese forces is the 81mm Type 97, which entered service in 1937. It is a relatively heavy and stable weapons platform, which the Japanese use to great effect to support their infantry.

Cost	35pts (Inexperienced), 50pts (Regular), 65pts (Veteran)
Team	3 men
Weapons	1 medium mortar
Options	- May add spotter for +10pts.
Special Rules	- Team Weapon - Indirect Fire - Fixed - HE(D6)

Heavy Mortar Team

The Japanese employ a number of mortars that are categorised as 'heavy' on account of their calibre and range, including the 90mm Type 94 and Type 97, as well as the 150mm Type 96 and Type 97, which fires a shell weighing a massive 25kg.

Cost	46pts (Inexperienced), 65pts (Regular), 84pts (Veteran)
Team	4 men
Weapons	1 heavy mortar
Options	- May add spotter for +10pts.
Special Rules	- Team Weapon - Fixed - Indirect Fire - HE(2D6)

ARTILLERY

Type 92 70mm Infantry Gun

The Type 92 infantry gun is a tiny weapon with a short barrel and split carriage that makes it an ideal lightweight support weapon that can be pulled by a horse or mule.

Cost	32pts (Inexperienced), 40pts (Regular), 48pts (Veteran)
Team	3 men
Weapons	1 light howitzer
Special Rules	- Gun Shield - Team Weapon - Fixed - Howitzer - Small HE(D3)

75mm Field Gun
(Type 41, Type 38, Type 90 and Type 95)

The Type 41 mountain gun is based on the German Krupp mountain gun and is the standard pack-artillery of the Japanese Army. The standard weapon, Type 90, has largely replaced the venerable Type 38 in regular service. The Type 90 has proved expensive and complicated to produce, heavy, and difficult to maintain. Problems with the Type 90 have led to the development of the shorter-ranged and less capable Type 95. The following entry can also be used to represent the Type 94 'Rentai Ho' mountain gun which is now mostly used as a regimental infantry gun.

Cost	60pts (Inexperienced), 75pts (Regular), 90pts (Veteran)
Team	4 men
Weapons	1 light howitzer
Options	- May add up to 2 crew for +5pts each.
Special Rules	- Gun Shield - Team Weapon - Fixed - Howitzer - HE(D6)

Type 91 105mm Field Gun

The Japanese field several types of medium-weight artillery of 105mm calibre, of which the Type 91 is typically assigned to field artillery regiments. It is a capable, modern and effective weapon which has been produced in large numbers.

Cost	68pts (Inexperienced), 85pts (Regular), 102pts (Veteran)
Team	6 men
Weapons	1 medium howitzer
Options	- May add Spotter for +10pts.
Special Rules	- Gun Shield - Team Weapon - Fixed - Howitzer - HE(2D6)

Type 4 Heavy Howitzer

The Type 4 150mm heavy howitzer appeared in 1914 and was obsolete at the beginning of the Second Sino–Japanese War in 1937. It lacked the range and mobility of more modern weapons of similar calibre such as the German heavy field guns used by the Chinese. The Type 96 is a more capable weapon, although it fires the same shells as the Type 4, and has become the standard heavy howitzer of the Japanese Army.

Cost	92pts (Inexperienced), 115pts (Regular), 138pts (Veteran)
Team	5 men
Weapons	1 heavy howitzer
Options	- May add up to 3 crew for +5pts each. - May add Spotter for +10pts.
Special Rules	- Gun Shield - Team Weapon - Fixed - Howitzer - HE(3D6)

ANTI-AIRCRAFT GUNS

The Japanese have a variety of large-calibre anti-aircraft guns, none of which really enter into the realm of the tabletop wargame. Smaller 20mm-calibre weapons were supplemented by pintle-mounted machine guns of various types.

Type 98 20mm AA Gun

The Type 98 is the most common automatic anti-aircraft cannon used by the Japanese. It is based on a Hotchkiss design and was introduced in 1938. A more sophisticated weapon is the Type 2 of 1942, based on the German Flak 38 with a central fire-control mechanism and sometimes fitted in a dual mount.

Cost	36pts (Inexperienced), 45pts (Regular), 54pts (Veteran)
Team	3 men
Weapons	1 light automatic cannon
Options	- May be upgraded to a Type 2 dual cannon for +30pts, increasing its shots from 2 to 4.
Special Rules	- Team Weapon - Fixed - Flak

Japanese Type 98 20mm anti-aircraft Gun

Prowling through the undergrowth, a Type 6 Scorpion walker hunts the enemy

ANTI-TANK GUNS

Tanks didn't dominate the war in the jungles of Southeast Asia or the Pacific as much as they did in the open steppes of Russia. The Japanese never developed specialised heavy anti-tank guns, although field artillery was often used against armour, and the lighter anti-tank guns available were capable of dealing with lightly armoured vehicles.

Type 94/Type 1 37mm Anti-Tank Gun

The Type 94 light anti-tank gun was introduced in 1936 and is known to the Japanese as an 'infantry rapid fire gun'. It is capable of firing both HE and AT shells and is widely used throughout Japanese forces. The Type 1 was introduced in 1941 and is an improved version of the Type 94 with a longer barrel but only very slightly enhanced performance.

Cost	40pts (Inexperienced), 50pts (Regular), 60pts (Veteran)
Team	3 men
Weapons	Light anti-tank gun
Special Rules	- Gun Shield - Team Weapon - Fixed

Imperial Japanese Army 47mm anti-tank gun

Type 1 47mm Anti-Tank Gun

The Type 1 47mm anti-tank gun was developed following the Japanese encounter with Russian armour and was the first indigenously developed dedicated anti-tank gun. It lacked the performance of other contemporary weapons of similar calibre, but was deemed sufficiently capable against lightly armoured tanks. By the time it was introduced in 1942, it was already outdated. The same gun is used as the main armament of the Type 97 Chi-Ha Shinhoto tank. It is also used by Japanese paratroopers – dropped disassembled in separate containers.

Cost	60pts (Inexperienced), 75pts (Regular), 90pts (Veteran)
Team	3 men
Weapons	Medium anti-tank gun
Special Rules	- Gun Shield - Team Weapon - Fixed

WALKERS

Japanese walker technology is based heavily on the multi-limbed technology provided by Germany, although the Japanese advances in miniaturisation and battery storage mean that they are working on a number of new directions for medium and heavy walkers. Technology exchanges with Germany mean that future walker developments by both countries are inevitable.

Japanese Sasori Scorpion Crawler

Type 6 'Sasori' light walker. (Ke-Ho Kei-Hokosensha)

The Type 6 light walker has been developed to replace armoured cars, tankettes and light tank destroyers. The ambition is to deploy a single walker platform that can go anywhere the infantry can, and deliver heavier fire support once it arrives. In this regard they have succeeded. The Type 6 Ke-Ho clearly owes its speed and agility to the German Spinne but combines this with a lower profile and quieter engine, making it an excellent recce vehicle. Nicknamed the Sasori ('scorpion') by its crews, the name is now commonly used by both Japanese and Allied soldiers. The earlier versions of the Type 6 were armed with a pair of MMGs for anti-infantry protection, but later versions mount an additional crewman and fixed heavy weapon at the rear of the walker.

Cost	95pts (Regular), 115pts (Veteran)
Weapons	2 forward-facing casement-mounted linked MMGs
Damage Value	7+
Options	- Add forward-facing casement mounted light anti-tank gun for +30pts. - Replace light anti-tank gun with a forward-facing casement mounted light compression cannon
Special Rules	- Recce - Agile - Walker

ASSAULT GUNS, TANK DESTROYERS AND TANKS

The Japanese did not produce any tanks of their own until 1929 and the first examples were versions of contemporary British and French models from Vickers, Renault and Carden-Loyd. Experience in Manchuria caused the Japanese to use Russian armour as a model. Heavy armour played a minor part in Japan's military strategy, and by the time her armies were obliged to face modern enemy tanks it was almost too late. Increasingly, more effective medium tanks are becoming available but they still suffer in comparison to those used by the Allies.

Type 3 Ho-Ni III Tank Destroyer

The original Ho-Ni was based on the chassis of the Chi-Ha and mounted a 75mm gun. The Ho-Ni III is an improvement on the original Ho-Ni with a completely enclosed superstructure.

Cost	112pts (Inexperienced), 140pts (Regular)
Weapons	1 casement-mounted forward-facing medium anti-tank gun
Damage Value	8+ (light tank)

Japanese Ho Ni MkIII tank destroyer

Type 4 Ho-Ro Assault Gun

The Ho-Ro is based on the chassis of the Chi-Ha and carries a 150mm howitzer on an open chassis.

Cost	124pts (Inexperienced), 155pts (Regular)
Weapons	1 forward-facing heavy howitzer
Damage Value	7+ (armoured carrier)
Special Rules	- Open-topped

Type 2 Ke-To Light Tank

The Type 2 Ke-To is based upon the Type 98 Ke-Ni, which it replaced after the Type 98's brief period of service proved it to be ineffective. It features an improved 37mm anti-tank gun in a larger turret.

Cost	100pts (Inexperienced), 125pts (Regular)
Weapons	1 turret-mounted light anti-tank gun, and 1 co-axial MMG
Damage Value	8+ (light tank)

Type 4 Ke-Nu Light Tank

The Type 4 Ke-Nu was a conversion of obsolete Ha-Go tanks created by retrofitting the larger Chi-Ha turret and gun – a low-velocity 54mm gun intended for close infantry support. Initially retained as a defensive vehicle for the Japanese mainland, as numbers have increased they are finding their way to the front lines in China and the Pacific islands.

Cost	92pts (Inexperienced), 115pts (Regular)
Weapons	1 turret-mounted light howitzer, 1 turret-mounted rear-facing MMG and 1 forward-facing hull-mounted MMG
Damage Value	7+ (armoured carrier)

Type 97-Kai Shinhoto Chi-Ha Medium Tank

In 1942 the Chi-Ha, Japan's standard medium tank, was up-gunned with a high-velocity 47mm anti-tank gun in a new and larger turret. This new version is known as the Type 97-Kai Shinhoto (meaning 'new turret'). As Rift-tech scientists developed the first compression cannons, the Chi-Ha chassis was used as a test bed for the early weapons, leading to a compression cannon-armed variant entering service in late 1946.

Cost	124pts (Inexperienced), 155pts (Regular), 186pts (Veteran)
Weapons	1 turret-mounted medium anti-tank gun, 1 turret-mounted rear-facing MMG and 1 forward-facing hull-mounted MMG
Damage Value	8+ (light tank)
Options	- Replace medium AT gun with light compression cannon for +10pts.

Type 3 Chi-Nu Medium Tank

Primarily designed to cope with the American M4 Sherman, the Chi-Nu was an improved version of the Type 97 Chi-Ha line. Its 75mm gun is one of the largest used on a Japanese tank. With the development of Rift-tech compression weapons, the Chi-Nu also received a modified turret to incorporate the new and heavier compression cannon being rushed into service. Deployed for the first time in early 1947, the heavier cannon has proved a potent weapon.

Cost	156pts (Inexperienced), 195pts (Regular)
Weapons	1 turret-mounted medium anti-tank gun, 1 turret-mounted rear-facing MMG and 1 forward-facing hull-mounted MMG
Damage Value	9+ (medium tank)
Options	- Replace medium AT gun with compression cannon for +40pts.

Type 3 Chi Nu medium tank

Shinhoto Chi Ha

TANKETTES AND ARMOURED CARS

The Japanese use small, lightly armoured tankettes in the same scouting and reconnaissance role as armoured cars – in fact, the Japanese designation for these tiny tanks literally means 'armoured car'. Wheeled armoured cars are used as well – and to differentiate them in this list we use the term 'tankette' for fully tracked vehicles and 'armoured car' for wheeled vehicles.

Type 87 Armoured Car

This lightly armoured vehicle is based on imported British Vickers Crossley. It is armed with two machine guns in a distinctive hemispherical turret. Mainly used by the SNLF, it is rarely seen on the front line and is largely used as a policing vehicle in annexed territories.

Cost	56pts (Inexperienced), 70pts (Regular), 84pts (Veteran)
Weapons	2 turret-mounted MMGs
Damage Value	7+ (armoured car)

Type 92 Tankette

The Type 92 Heavy Armoured Car is, despite its name, a fully tracked tankette. Although, in reality, it is a light tank in all but name. It is used by cavalry formations and is most extensively deployed on the Manchuria and Korean fronts.

Cost	72pts (Inexperienced), 90 (Regular), 108pts (Veteran)
Weapons	1 turret-mounted HMG and 1 forward-facing hull-mounted MMG.
Damage Value	7+ (armoured car)
Special Rules	- Recce

Type 94 Tankette

The Type 94 tankette, or TK, was developed for the infantry divisions of the IJA. It is not a replacement for the Type 92, which was created for the cavalry divisions. The Type 94 is intended to provide the infantry with a vehicle suitable for scouting, reconnaissance and communications, as well as a rapid infantry support weapon. It weighs about 3.5 tons.

Cost	56pts (Inexperienced), 70pts (Regular), 84pts (Veteran)
Weapons	1 turret-mounted MMG
Damage Value	7+ (armoured car)
Special Rules	- Recce

Type 97 Te-Ke Tankette

The Type 97 tankette has been designed as a replacement for the Type 94 in the reconnaissance and support role. It is heavier, at nearly 5 tons, and carries a 37mm gun in its tiny one-man turret.

Cost	76pts (Inexperienced), 95 (Regular), 114pts (Veteran)
Weapons	1 turret-mounted light anti-tank gun
Damage Value	7+ (armoured car)
Special Rules	- Recce - One-man turret (it is always necessary to take an order test when issuing an Advance order, even if not pinned) - Low-velocity light anti-tank gun (the main weapon has a PEN value of +3 instead of the usual +4)

ANTI-AIRCRAFT VEHICLES

A variety of different vehicles are used to mount anti-aircraft weapons. The 20mm automatic cannon is in general use and could also be trained against ground targets.

Type 98 AA Truck

This is a Type 98 20mm automatic cannon mounted on the back of a Type 94 or (later) a Type 96 six-wheeled truck.

Cost	40pts (Inexperienced), 50pts (Regular), 60pts (Veteran)
Weapons	1 platform-mounted light autocannon with 360-degree arc of fire
Damage Value	6+ (soft-skin)
Special Rules	-Flak

Japanese Type 94 tankette

TRANSPORTS AND TOWS

The Japanese have suffered from a lack of transports throughout the war. The Japanese soldier is expected to compensate for this by his hardiness. When transports are available, the soldiers are packed in tight – in game terms, we have increased the transport capacity of many vehicles to represent this and to ensure that full-strength basic infantry squads can fit on board.

General Purpose Trucks

Japanese trucks are inclined to be narrow to suit local roads and have high ground clearance to cope with uneven surfaces. The Toyota GB and KB types have been produced in large numbers. Type 94 6x4 trucks also provide the chassis for an armoured car and are relatively heavy – comparable to a British Bedford QLD. The Type 1 Toyota truck of 1941 is an almost exact copy of a 1939 Chevrolet. Many trucks of different kinds have been captured from the enemy and pressed into service. All of these medium-sized trucks are comparable in terms of capacity and performance and are represented with the following stats.

Cost	33pts (Inexperienced), 41pts (Regular), 49pts (Veteran)
Weapons	None
Damage Value	6+ (soft-skin)
Transport	Up to 13 men
Tow	Light Howitzers; light or medium anti-tank guns; Light anti-aircraft guns
Options	- May have a pintle-mounted MMG covering the forward arc for +15pts.

Light Trucks

Lighter types of trucks included the Type 97 Nissan, which was partly based on the pre-war Graham-Paige design. These smaller vehicles have about half the capacity of a standard general purpose truck.

Cost	25pts (Inexperienced), 31pts (Regular), 37pts (Veteran)
Weapons	None
Damage Value	6+ (soft-skin)
Transport	Up to 8 men
Tow	Light howitzers; light or medium anti-tank guns; light anti-aircraft guns
Options	- May have a pintle-mounted MMG covering the forward arc for +15pts.

Type 1 Ho-Ha Half-Track

The Ho-Ha is an open-topped armoured half-track based loosely upon the German Hanomag, which it broadly resembles. It was introduced in 1944 and has mostly been used in China and the Philippines.

Cost	89pts (Inexperienced), 111pts (Regular), 133pts (Veteran)
Weapons	1 hull-mounted MMG covering the left arc, 1 hull-mounted MMG covering the right arc, 1 pintle-mounted MMG covering the rear arc
Damage Value	7+ (armoured carrier)
Transport	Up to 13 men
Tow	Light or medium howitzers; light or medium anti-tank guns; light anti-aircraft guns
Special Rules	Open-topped

Type 95 Kurogane

The Kurogane ('black metal') was a purpose-built four-wheel drive car that fulfils a similar role to the German Kubelwagen or US jeep. The Japanese also make use of numerous civilian cars of similar capacity and overall performance, if somewhat less suited to the rigours of military use.

Cost	18pts (Inexperienced), 23pts (Regular), 28pts (Veteran)
Weapons	None
Damage Value	6+ (soft-skin)
Transport	Up to 4
Tow	None
Options	- May have a pintle-mounted MMG with 360-degree arc of fire for +15pts, losing all transport capacity.

Type 95 Kurogane Field Car

Type 98 So-Da Carrier

The So-Da carrier is an unarmed version of the Type 97 Te-Ke tankette and is designed as an armoured ammunition carrier. It is commonly used as a tow but can also carry infantry.

Cost	45pts (Inexperienced), 57pts (Regular), 68pts (Veteran)
Weapons	None
Damage Value	7+ (armoured carrier)
Transport	Up to 6 men
Tow	Light or medium howitzers; light or medium anti-tank guns; light anti-aircraft guns
Special Rules	- May have a pintle-mounted MMG with 360-degree arc of fire for +15pts, losing all transport capacity.

Type 98 Ro-Ke Prime Mover

The 6-ton Ro-Ke prime mover is a fully tracked heavy artillery tractor introduced in 1939. It is used to tow heavy guns such as the 105 and 150mm howitze

Cost	14pts (Inexperienced), 17pts (Regular), 20pts (Veteran)
Weapons	None
Damage Value	6+ (soft-skin carrier)
Transport	Up to 6 men
Tow	Any anti-tank gun, howitzer or anti-aircraft gun
Special Rules	- Slow

Tank Recovery Tractor

All nations use variations of the humble tractor to recover damaged combat vehicles. The variety is endless, from commandeered agricultural machines to military models with lightly armoured cabs and weaponry for self-defence.

Cost	10pts (Inexperienced), 12pts (Regular), 14pts (Veteran)
Weapons	None
Damage Value	6+ (soft-skin carrier)
Transport	Up to 6 men
Tow	- May add a pintle-mounted forward-facing MMG for +15pts.
Special Rules	- ARV

A Type 6 Ke-Ho light walker traverses jungle terrain

FINLAND

This force list represents the free Finnish forces fighting as part of the SS Freiwilligen Division Nord-Ost and its Resistance allies. It uses the reinforced platoon force structure as normal.

Where a unit entry instructs you to select from the German Army List in the core rulebook, use the points and options as listed there. The unit narrative is added here to maintain the Finnish national flavour of the list.

ARMY SPECIAL RULES

These national rules apply to Finnish troops only. Do not use the national rules for Germany, even if using troop entries from the core rulebook to select your Finnish force.

Sisu

Whilst the Finnish Army has been disbanded, the determination of Finnish soldiers is fuelled by a desire for revenge on the Soviet invaders and they retain their bravery, ferocity and ability to adapt in combat. When below 50% of their starting strength, infantry squads (not teams) are upgraded to the next higher quality level. Therefore Inexperienced troops become Regular and Regular become Veteran. This applies to both morale and Damage values.

Finnish anti-tank rifle

Trained Huntsmen

Most men in Finland are trained to shoot and hunt from an early age. When firing from Ambush, any troops using a rifle or anti-tank rifle receive +1 to hit.

Motti

The Finnish are expert at encircling and splitting enemy forces into smaller, more manageable sizes. Using terrain such as lakes and forests to divide opponents, the Finns will also allow elements of the enemy to escape if it allowed the trapped remainder to be dealt with safely. Finnish forces do not suffer the -1 modifier when testing to enter the table from an outflanking move.

Schurzen Armoured Skirts

If a tank or vehicle has the Schurzen upgrade, then anti-tank rifles and shaped charges do not get the +1 PEN bonus for hitting it in the side.

Hitler's Buzzsaw

Finnish units and vehicles equipped with light and medium machine guns fire one extra shot (5 for LMG and 6 for a MMG).

TYPES OF UNIT

1	Infantry	Headquarters units
		Infantry squads
		Infantry teams
2	Artillery	Anti-tank guns
		Field artillery
3	Vehicles	Tanks
		Tank destroyers
		Walkers
		Armoured cars
		Self-propelled artillery
		Anti-aircraft vehicles
		Transports and tows

HEADQUARTERS

Each platoon is centred upon a core that includes a headquarter unit in the form of a First or Second Lieutenant. Other HQ units can be added to the force, including higher-ranking officers, as well as medical units and supporting observers.

Officer

Most junior officers are trained to German standards of self-reliance and initiative, already a natural trait in many Finnish veterans. An officer unit consists of the officer himself and may include up to two other men acting as his immediate attendants.

As per German entry in Konflikt '47 rulebook, but add following special rule for no cost:

Ski Troops (ignore movement penalties for snow and other winter conditions)

Medic

The field medic presents wounded soldiers with his best chance of surviving serious injury and can return lightly wounded soldiers back to combat in short order. Junior medical staff – such as stretcher-bearers – may accompany a medic.

As per German entry in Konflikt '47 rulebook, but add following special rule for no cost:

Ski Troops (ignore movement penalties for snow and other winter conditions)

Forward Observer

Forward observers are the officers responsible for co-ordinating the attack of artillery batteries or aircraft strikes. They are likely to be accompanied by a radio operator and possibly an assistant.

As per German entry in Konflikt '47 rulebook, but add following special rule for no cost:

Ski Troops (ignore movement penalties for snow and other winter conditions)

INFANTRY SQUADS AND TEAMS

Rifle Squad

By 1947, equipped with proven German equipment, the standard Finnish infantry squad is well trained, well motivated and well armed. Combined with a natural tenacity and high morale, Finish infantry are a threat to every Russian unit they encounter.

Cost	50pts (Regular), 65pts (Veteran)
Team	1 NCO and 4 men
Weapons	Rifle
Options	- Add up to 4 additional men at +10pts (Regular) or +13pts (Veteran) each. - The NCO and up to 2 additional men may replace their rifles with SMGs at +3pts each. - Up to 2 men may replace their rifles with an LMG for +20pts, for each LMG another soldier becomes the loader. - Up to 2 men can have a panzerfaust for +5pts each. - The entire squad can have anti-tank grenades for +2pts per model if unit not equipped with panzerfausts. - The entire squad can be equipped with skis for +1pt per model.
Special Rules	- Tank Hunter (if grenades taken) - Ski Troops (ignore movement penalties for snow and other winter conditions)

Jääkäri Falcon Squad

Jääkäri or Jaegers are experienced light infantry and are highly mobile using Rift-tech designed Falcon armour to outflank and out-manoeuvre slower Russian formations.

Cost	130pts (Veteran)
Team	1 NCO and 4 men
Weapons	Assault rifle
Options	- Add up to 3 additional men with assault rifles at +26pts (Veteran) each. - Any model may replace their assault rifle with an SMG for -2pts each. - Up to two men can have a panzerfaust for +5pts each.
Special Rules	Flight Resilient

Kaukopartio Recon Squad [Max 1 Per Platoon]

These soldiers are handpicked from the best of the Finnish military and include former world-class athletes and marksmen. All are survival specialists and are each trained as medics, radio operators and paratroopers. They operate behind enemy lines, sowing destruction and terror as both commandos and intelligence gatherers.

Cost	115pts (Veteran)
Team	1 NCO and 4 men
Weapons	SMG and anti-tank grenades
Options	- Add up to 4 additional men with SMGs at +23pts (Veteran) each. - Any model may have a rifle in addition to their SMG for +1pt per model, they may only fire one weapon per turn. - The entire squad can be equipped with skis for +1pt per model.
Special Rules	- Tank Hunter - Ski Troops (ignore movement penalties for snow and other winter conditions) - Medic (squad members always count as having a medic within 6") - Stubborn - Deep Strike (when outflanking in a scenario, may enter from any board edge)

Finnish Rifle Squad

Sissi Recon Squad [Max 2 Per Platoon]

Sissi recon troops operate behind enemy lines, snatching prisoners and disrupting enemy lines of communication. Comprised of the most experienced and capable soldiers, they are used to conducting dangerous missions where their hunting and fighting skills can be put to good use.

Finnish Sissi Squad

Cost	70pts (Veteran)
Team	1 NCO and 4 men
Weapons	Rifle
Options	- Add up to 4 additional men at +14pts (Veteran) each. - Any models may replace their rifles with SMGs at +3pts each. - 1 man may replace his rifle with an LMG for +20pts, another soldier becomes the loader. - Up to 2 men can have a panzerfaust for +5pts each. - The entire squad can be equipped with skis for +1pt per model. - The entire squad may be Tough Fighters for +1pt per model.
Special Rules	Hunters - Tough Fighter (if taken) - Ski Troops (ignore movement penalties for snow and other winter conditions)

SS Freiwillingen Shocktrooper Squad

The most committed members of the German-trained SS Freiwillingen Division that show genuine commitment to the political ideals of Germany are often drawn together for additional political training. They are then formed into new Shocktrooper units to maximise their impact on the front line. Well equipped, and wearing the latest body armour, they often form the spearhead of assault operations.

Cost	90pts (Regular)
Team	1 NCO and 4 men
Weapons	Assault rifle
Options	- Add up to 5 additional men with assault rifles for +18pts each. - Up to 2 men can have an LMG for +10pts each, for each LMG another man becomes its loader. - Up to 4 men can have a panzerfaust in addition to other weapons for +5pts each. - Up to 2 men can have rifle grenades for +20pts each.
Special Rules	- Tough - IR Vision - Stubborn

Heavy Infantry Squad [Max 1 Per Platoon]

The Finnish have not embraced the use of Heavy Armoured Infantry as a regular unit tactic, but a small cadre of political, loyal troops have been issued the armour to provide an additional tactical option when assaulting heavily defended positions.

As per German entry in Konflikt '47 rulebook, page 129.

Shreckwulfen Squad

Whilst Finnish volunteers for the Rift-tech experimental super-soldier programme are not common, a significant number have stepped forward to further the cause of liberating their country. What criteria the volunteers need to meet to be accepted in to the programme is highly classified, but Finnish Shreckwulfen are certainly part of the operation to rid the country of Soviet invaders.

As per German entry in Konflikt '47 rulebook, page 131.

Shreckwulfen

Nachtjäger Squad

A very small number of the Finnish volunteers that step forward for the German super-soldier programme emerge from the Dresden laboratories as the fearsome Nachtjägers. These troops are used to harass and terrorise the Soviet garrisons across Finland, a task they are perfectly suited for.

As per German entry in Konflikt '47 rulebook, page 133.

Partisan Squad

On many operations the regular Finnish forces make use of local partisans and Resistance fighters who know both the ground and the target far better than the soldiers. These partisans are hardy, brave and often former Finnish soldiers. They are usually equipped with captured Soviet equipment or weapons supplied by the German Army.

Cost	35pts (Inexperienced), 50pts (Regular)
Team	1 leader (NCO) and 4 men
Weapons	Rifle
Options	- Add up to 15 additional riflemen at +7pts (Inexperienced) or +10pts (Regular) each. - Up to 5 models may replace their rifle with an SMG for +3pts each. - 1 man may replace his rifle with an LMG for +20pts, another man becomes the loader. - 1 man may have a panzerfaust for +5pts. - The entire squad can have anti-tank grenades for +2pts per model. - The entire squad can be equipped with skis for +1pt per model.
Special Rules	- Tank Hunter (if grenades taken) - Ski Troops (ignore movement penalties for snow and other winter conditions)

Medium Machine Gun Team

The Finnish are equipped with the excellent German MG42 or MG44 machine gun, and are well trained in its use. The weapon is used both as an LMG within infantry squads and as an MMG when tripod-mounted.

As per German entry in Konflikt '47 rulebook.

Flamethrower Team

The Finns utilise flamethrowers as part of their terror operations to remove the Soviets from their country. Few of the original Italian Lanciafiamme Spalleggiabile-35s remain in service, but German replacements are used.

Cost	50pts (Regular), 65pts (Veteran)
Team	2 men
Weapons	1 infantry flamethrower
Options	- May have skis for +2pts.
Special Rules	- Team Weapon - Flamethrower - Ski Troops (ignore movement penalties for snow and other winter conditions)

Finnish Sniper team

Sniper Team

Using the purpose built Finnish M28-30 rifle with specially crafted ammunition, Finnish snipers are exceptionally effective.

Cost	60pts (Regular), 80pts (Veteran)
Team	2 men
Weapons	1 rifle
Options	- May have skis for +2pts.
Special Rules	- Team Weapon - Hunter - Sniper - Ski Troops (ignore movement penalties for snow and other winter conditions)

Light Mortar Team

The Finnish use German mortars in several calibres, the most common of which is the shortened 80mm infantry mortar. This is basically a close-range support weapon that can easily be carried and used by infantry.

Cost	35pts (Regular), 46pts (Veteran)
Team	2 men
Weapons	1 light mortar
Options	- May have skis for +2pts.
Special Rules	- Team Weapon - Indirect Fire - HE(D3) - Ski Troops (ignore movement penalties for snow and other winter conditions)

Medium Mortar Team

The standard Finnish medium mortar is the German 80mm Granatwerfer 34. It is a very effective and accurate weapon that can provide long-range fire support.

Cost	50pts (Regular), 65pts (Veteran)
Team	3 men
Weapons	1 medium mortar
Options	- May add spotter for +10pts.
Special Rules	- Team Weapon - Indirect Fire - Fixed - HE(D6)

Finnish Medium Mortar team

Heavy Mortar Team

The heavy mortar used is the German 120mm calibre Granatwerfer 42. It is a close copy of captured Russian mortars and has been developed to give infantry an even longer range and heavier weight of shot than the 80mm mortar.

Cost	65pts (Regular), 84pts (Veteran)
Team	4 men
Weapon	1 heavy mortar
Options	- May add spotter for +10pts.
Special Rules	- Team Weapon - Fixed - Indirect Fire - HE(2D6)

Panzerschreck Team

As per German entry in Konflikt '47 rulebook, page 129.

Anti-Tank Rifle Team

As per Heavy Sniper Team in the Konflikt '47 rulebook, 130.

Finnish Panzershreck Team

ARTILLERY AND ANTI-TANK GUNS

Never particularly well equipped with artillery, the Finnish reliance on captured Soviet guns has been replaced by a steady supply of German artillery pieces (although this is often still supplemented by the occasional captured weapon). Without the logistical capacity to support large numbers of artillery, heavy artillery is not currently in service within the Finnish SS Freiwilligen Division.

37mm PaK 36

Although considered obsolete by the Germans, the relatively light and mobile PaK 36 is considered a useful weapon by the Finnish who use it to ambush Soviet supply and relief columns.

Cost	50pts (Regular), 60pts (Veteran)
Team	3 men
Weapon	Light anti-tank gun
Options	- The crew may have skis and the gun placed on a sled for +4pts.
Special Rules	- Gun Shield - Team Weapon - Fixed

75mm PaK 40

The PaK 40 is the standard Finnish anti-tank gun of this period. It is a heavy but effective weapon capable of destroying any Soviet tank.

Cost	110pts (Regular), 132pts (Veteran)
Team	4 men
Weapon	Heavy anti-tank gun
Special Rules	- Gun Shield - Team Weapon - Fixed

Finnish PaK 40

Light Artillery

The Finnish employ a number of light artillery batteries, being able to move them relatively swiftly to support their operations. Although the models vary, these guns are used for close support and are light enough to be manhandled by their crews.

Cost	50pts (Regular), 60pts (Veteran)
Team	3 men
Weapons	1 light howitzer
Options	May add Spotter for +10pts.
Special Rules	- Gun Shield - Team Weapon - Fixed - Howitzer - HE(D6)

Medium Artillery

An under-strength artillery regiment of 105mm guns forms part of the Finnish Division. Slower to move and more vulnerable to Soviet counter-attacks, they are not used regularly on raid or ambush operations but are utilised in more substantial engagements.

Cost	75pts (Regular), 90pts (Veteran)
Team	4 men
Weapons	1 medium howitzer
Options	May add Spotter for +10pts.
Special Rules	- Gun Shield - Team Weapon - Fixed - Howitzer - HE(2D6)

TANKS AND ASSAULT GUNS

The Finnish SS Freiwilligen Division contains a full regiment of armour, although they are mostly older and un-needed vehicles passed on by German quartermasters. The regiment contains a battalion of Pz IV tanks and two battalions of tank destroyers, a lighter unit of StuG III/IVs and a heavier formation of Jagdpanzers that includes a handful of Jagdpanthers.

Panzer IV

The Panzer IV remains a stalwart performer and although being superseded by newer designs, was the obvious choice to equip the new Finnish units. Its main armament is capable of penetrating most Soviet tanks, although it will struggle against the newer Russian heavy tanks. After repeated Finnish requests, a few Panzer IV tanks in the battalion have been upgraded with the latest Rift-tech weaponry in the form of the Schwerefeld Projektor.

Cost	188pts (Inexperienced), 235pts (Regular), 282pts (Veteran)
Weapons	1 turret-mounted heavy anti-tank gun with co-axial MMG and one forward-facing hull-mounted MMG
Damage value	9+ (medium tank)
Options	- May have Schurzen armour skirts for +10pts. - May replace heavy anti-tank gun and co-axial MMG with turret-mounted Schwerefeld Projektor for -5pts (Regular) and -2pts (Veteran)

Jagdpanzer IV

The Jagdpanzer IV was developed in 1943 as a tank destroyer based on the Panzer IV chassis. Its frontal armour was thicker than a Panzer IV, and with its low profile and powerful gun it has proved a successful weapon that continues to serve German forces. As newer models are produced with the same 75mm gun as the Panther, several of the older models have been transferred to the Finnish Division.

Cost	270pts (Regular), 324pts (Veteran)
Weapons	1 casement-mounted forward-facing heavy anti-tank gun and forward-facing hull-mounted MMG
Damage value	9+ (medium tank)
Options	- May have Schurzen armour skirts for +10pts.
Special Rules	- The Jagdpanzer's heavy frontal armour has a rating of +1 giving it the same frontal value as a heavy tank (10+).

Finnish 105mm Artillery

Sturmi STUG III/IV

The Sturmgeschutz ('assault gun') was developed as an infantry support weapon based on the Panzer III and Panzer IV chassis, and continues to be produced in large numbers in Germany. Its low cost and ease of manufacture make it an easy choice to equip the ever-increasing Finnish forces.

Cost	230pts (Regular), 276pts (Veteran)
Weapons	1 casement-mounted forward-facing heavy antitank gun and remotely operated MMG with 360-degree arc of fire
Damage value	9+ (medium tank)
Options	- May add a forward-facing co-axial MMG for +15pts. - May have Schurzen armour skirts for +10pts.

Finnish Sturmi StuG III

Jagdpanther

The Jagdpanther tank destroyer is based on the Panther chassis and combines that tank's excellent mobility with a hard-hitting KwK 43 88mm gun as used in the Tiger II. This powerful gun is mounted into an extended front glacis that created a heavily armoured casement for the crew. With German heavy armour production moving back to turreted tanks and walkers, a small number of Jagdpanthers were given to the SS Freiwilligen Division to provide heavy anti-tank firepower.

Cost	390pts (Regular), 468pts (Veteran)
Weapons	1 hull mounted forward-facing super-heavy antitank gun and 1 forward-facing hull-mounted MMG
Damage value	10+ (heavy tank)

WALKERS

Spinne Light Panzermech

Combining the agility of an infantryman with the armour and firepower of a heavily built armoured car, the Spinne ('spider') is almost the perfect recce vehicle for the rough terrain of Finland. The Spinne has been adopted by the Finnish as the raiding vehicle of choice for long-range raids against Soviet columns and garrisons. The Spinne also performs traditional recce tasks and has replaced armoured cars throughout the SS Freiwilligen Division.

Cost	125pts (Regular), 145pts (Veteran)
Weapons	Turret-mounted light AT gun and co-axial light autocannon.
Damage value	7+ (light walker)
Options	- Replace light autocannon with a small vehicle flamethrower (range 12", 2D6-1 hits) and remove the Open-topped and Flak special rules for +30pts.
Special Rules	- Walker - Open-topped - Agile - Flak - Recce (dual-direction steering)

German Flammespinne

Zeus Heavy Panzermech

The Zeus panzermech was built to operate as a tank hunter in difficult terrain and is therefore well suited to much of the terrain in Finland. The number of Zeus heavy panzermechs in Finnish service is kept a closely guarded secret, but they have certainly had an impact in Finland's increasingly aggressive operations against the Russian occupiers.

Cost	410pts (Regular), 500pts (Veteran)
Weapons	1 turret-mounted super-heavy anti-tank gun and 1 forward-facing light auto-cannon. 1 pintle-mounted MMG
Damage value	10+ (super-heavy walker)
Special Rules	- Walker - Slow - Tough (front arc only)

TRANSPORTS AND TOWS
Truck

The terrain the Finnish Division often chooses to operate over makes the use of trucks and lighter wheeled vehicles difficult, but as with any force, the availability of utility trucks means they can be used to transport infantry when practical. Many models have been pressed into service, whether German, Finnish or Russian.

Cost:	39pts (Regular), 47pts (Veteran)
Weapons	None
Damage value	6+ (soft-skin)
Transport	Up to 12 men
Tow	Light howitzers; light or medium anti-tank guns
Options	- May have pintle-mounted MMG with 360-degree arc of fire for +15pts.

German Zeus Heavy Panzermech

Tank Recovery Tractor

All nations use variations of the humble tractor to recover damaged combat vehicles. The variety is endless, from commandeered agricultural machines to military models with lightly armoured cabs and weaponry for self-defence.

Cost	10pts (Inexperienced), 12pts (Regular), 14pts (Veteran)
Weapons	None
Damage value	6+ (soft-skin)
Options	- May add a pintle-mounted forward-facing MMG for +15pts.
Special Rules	- ARV

Bergepanther

Provided to the Finns in small numbers, the Bergepanther is able to recover all but the heaviest of fighting vehicles. The scarcity of armoured vehicles within the Finnish Division ensures every effort is made to recover damaged tanks and walkers from the battlefield.

Cost	102pts (Inexperienced), 128pts (Regular), 154pts (Veteran)
Weapons	1 pintle-mounted forward-facing MMG
Damage value	9+ (medium tank)
Options	- May replace MMG with forward facing 20mm light automatic cannon for +20pts.
Special Rules	- ARV - Open-topped - Heavy front armour (Damage value is 10+ in the front arc)

A hull-down Zeus targets advancing American armour

NEW SCENARIOS AND RULES

The following pages introduce a new set of scenarios written with the *Konflikt '47* battlefield in mind. As such, you'll find the option to play dawn-, dusk- or night-based scenarios which will allow units with IR Vision to add another dimension to gameplay.

NEW SCENARIO RULES

The following new scenario rules are common to multiple scenarios and are gathered together here to save repeating them throughout the scenario descriptions.

DECIDING THE SIZE OF THE GAME

Before the battle can begin it is necessary that the players agree how big a game they are going to play. Begin by agreeing the number of requisition points available for the game; the more points the bigger and more powerful the army and the longer the game may take to play. For example, players might agree to play a 1,250 points game, meaning that each side fields up to a maximum of 1,250 requisition points.

For practical purposes, we recommend 1,250 requisition points per side for a standard-sized game. Later on, the rules for different scenarios assume that games are being fought using this standard size. Of course, that does not mean games cannot be played with more or fewer points!

NIGHT FIGHTING

The following rules deal with the limited visibility and uncertainty caused by night operations. These rules present a layer of complexity to the game and will slightly slow down the speed of gameplay, but they create a different gaming experience and present new tactical challenges. The increased number of units in *Konflikt '47* with the ability to see in the dark provides some interesting scenario variations; however, forces with little access to IR Vision may be significantly disadvantaged against those that have. Players may wish to adjust the requisition points available to each side dependant on IR Vision available in their force. Generally, a Soviet player should have more points than their opponent if playing a non-Soviet opponent. If neither side has actually selected any units with IR Vision, obviously there is no need to alter anything!

Night and darkness comes in many forms with varied light levels. Four variations are presented here. If players wish to fight a scenario at night, they should decide before playing which variation they are going to use, unless the use of night fighting rules is specified in the scenario rules.

In a *Dawn Assault*, the game begins in darkness with the reduced visibility rules, but you must roll a die at the beginning of each turn after the first, adding the current turn number to the result. On a modified total of 8 or more, the reduced visibility rules immediately cease to apply and visibility returns to normal for the rest of the game.

Tooth and Claw - Shreckwulfen and Ursus rip into each other

In a *Longest Day* game, you begin with normal visibility, but must roll a die at the beginning of each turn after the first and add the current turn to the result. If the modified result is 8 or more, the reduced visibility rules immediately begin to apply and last for the rest of the game.

In a *Flare* game, the action takes place at night, with reduced visibility rules in play throughout, but you must roll a die at the start of each turn after the first. On a roll of 4 or more, a powerful flare goes up (or a series of smaller flares are fired from nearby mortars or artillery) and visibility is normal for that turn only. Roll again at the start of the next turn as above.

For a *Night* game, the reduced visibility rules apply throughout.

Reduced Visibility

When you are determining whether a unit is able to see a target at night, first follow the normal rules for line of sight. Weapons that do not rely on LoS (such as the Soviet Zvukovoy Proyektor) need not make a spotting roll to fire. If the target would be visible, then start the normal shooting or assault procedure and declare the target. Then, before the first 'target reacts' step, you must take a spotting roll for the acting unit to see whether they can actually identify the target through the darkness. Roll 2D6 and add or subtract any of the modifiers listed below that apply, down to a minimum of 2.

VISIBILITY MODIFIERS	
The target has Fire, Advance, Run or no order die	+6
The target has a muzzle flash marker on it	+6
The target has a Down order die on it	-3
The target is a small unit	-6
The target is a vehicle	+6
The acting unit has the IR Vision special rule*	+18

* This is an optional variation of the standard wording of the IR Vision special rule aimed at making the rule more balanced in the context of these visibility rules. If players wish, they can ignore this modifier and allow IR Vision-enabled models to see normally at all times under the reduced visibility rules. Agree this before the game!

If the modified roll is equal or higher than the distance (in inches) between the acting unit and the target then the target is visible and the firing or assault sequence continues as normal.

If the total is lower than the distance to the target, the acting unit cannot shoot or assault the target and its action ends immediately (the acting unit's order die is left as it was declared), imagine the unit scanning the darkness and second-guessing what they thought they saw.

As the visibility range is determined prior to the first reaction opportunity in each case, it may be that the target unit cannot see the unit shooting at it or about to assault it, meaning the reaction opportunity is lost.

Soviet Mammoth Heavy Walker

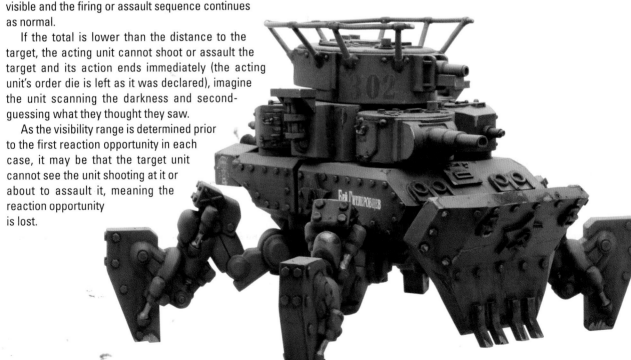

Muzzle Flashes

Firing weapons at night is a sure-fire way of revealing your positions to the enemy. To represent this, when a unit fires any weaponry, it must be marked with a muzzle flash marker (a coin or other token). This token makes the unit more visible, as shown in the visibility modifiers table. The marker remains with the unit until it receives its next order die. It is possible that a unit may not actually fire its weapons after a Fire or Advance order due to the reduced visibility modifiers; in this case, no muzzle flash marker is received.

Fires

Burning vehicles, buildings or other features illuminate a surprisingly wide area at night and anyone near them is very likely to get spotted. Count any unit within 6" of a burning vehicle, building or terrain feature as having a muzzle flash token on them, even if they haven't fired.

Reactions in Reduced Visibility

It is entirely possible that a unit will want to react to being shot at or assaulted, and most reactions are permitted without restrictions. However, should a unit wish to conduct a firefight or stand and shoot reaction, they must make a spotting roll to see if they can see the models attacking them. This spotting test is carried out before an assaulting unit moves. If the reacting unit fails to roll a high enough distance, and therefore fails to spot its attackers, it may not make a reaction. This does not count as a failed reaction.

Indirect Fire

If a weapon with Indirect Fire has zeroed in on a target, there is no need to make further spotting rolls to continue firing at the same target, simply roll to hit on a 2+ as normal.

Forward Air and Artillery Observers

When an artillery observer call in a barrage, it does not get a muzzle flash token as the observer is not firing a weapon. When calling in a barrage, the observer does not need to make a spotting roll, but can instead place the marker anywhere on the table, as he would be relying on maps and noise/gun flashes rather than direct observation of targets. However, to simulate the increased chances of something going wrong, you suffer a -1 on the artillery or smoke barrage charts (to a minimum of 1). Air strikes cannot be called at all at night (or in a scenario using these rules), making forward air observers quite useless.

DUG IN

Every soldier understands the benefits of digging in whenever time allows, and it doesn't take long for well-motivated infantry to disappear into the ground given a short amount of time and a decent entrenching tool. Where a scenario indicates the dug in rules are being applied, troops may start the game in foxholes and trenches. Units starting the game dug in may also be subject to the hidden set-up rules as well. Dug in units are still placed on the table in the normal way, but should be marked in some fashion to show their protected status. Being dug in does not provide any protection from a preparatory bombardment.

Dug-In Infantry and Artillery

A dug-in unit counts as Down when shot at (-1 to be hit and only suffer half HE hits); if the unit then is given a Down order or reaction, the modifiers double (-2 to be hit, only suffer one quarter HE hits). Being dug in offers no benefits during hand-to-hand combat but gives the targets the Down benefit during point-blank shooting. Units remain dug in until they receive an Advance or Run order, or are forced to consolidate away from their position in an assault.

Dug-In Vehicles

A vehicle may start the game dug in, and counts as in hard cover when shot at. It may also count the 'immobilised' damage result as 'crew stunned'. The nature of the defensive works required to protect an armoured vehicle means that the vehicle may not move for the duration of the game.

Dug In and Hidden Set-Up

A unit can be both dug in and use hidden set-up providing it satisfies the deployment restrictions for both. The hidden set-up rule takes precedence until it no longer applies; the dug-in unit does gain the additional protection of counting as Down against HE fire while hidden. Once the hidden rule no longer applies, the unit remains dug in until it moves as described above.

Dug In vs Tank Assault

A foxhole or trench can provide limited protection from vehicles passing over or nearby if it's properly constructed. Dug-in units automatically pass their morale check when assaulted by a vehicle but are not moved aside; however, if the vehicle ends its movement on top of any dug-in models, these are removed as casualties and the unit receives a pin marker and must take a morale check as required.

NEW SCENARIOS

THE BATTLE SCENARIOS

These scenarios supplement those in the main *Konflikt '47* rule book. They can be used to add flavour and variety to your games or can be incorporated into a narrative campaign to add additional flavour.

These scenarios have been worked out to provide a fair but varied challenge to both sides. None require any particular scenery or table set-up; they can be played with any forces or terrain. The use of night fighting rules will favour certain forces and units over others, so some consideration or consultation between players may be necessary if playing in a more competitive environment.

Players can simply pick a scenario to play, or roll a die at the start of the game and consult the updated scenario chart as follows:

BATTLE SCENARIOS CHART		
Die Roll 1	**Die Roll 2**	**Scenario**
1–3 (original scenarios)	1	Envelopment
	2	Maximum Attrition
	3	Point Defence
	4	Hold Until Relieved
	5	Top Secret
	6	Demolition
4–6 (new scenarios)	1	Night Raid
	2	Feint
	3	Delay
	4	Meeting Engagement
	5	Relief-in-Place
	6	Reconnaissance in Force

SCENARIO 1: NIGHT RAID

Utilising the cover of darkness, a raiding force advances silently on an unsuspecting enemy position. The raiding troops will have to use speed and surprise to inflict maximum damage on the in-place enemy force before it can reinforce its position and counter-attack to push back the raiders.

Forces

This scenario is designed to be played with equal points values on both sides.

The defender splits their force into two halves with up to half their units as the in-place force and the remaining portion starting the game in reserve (see Reserves in the Konflikt '47 rulebook, page 122). These will form the counter-attacking force, intent on driving the raiding force back.

The attacker's force, due to the covert approach to the raid, may not field any vehicles (including walkers) in their initial deployment. Any such vehicles must start the game in reserve. The attacker may hold as much of their force as they wish in reserve. If the attacking force contains no vehicles they may deploy their entire force on the table.

Set-Up

Both players roll a die. The highest scorer decides whether to be the attacker or the defender.

Deployment

The defender picks a side of the table and sets up no more than half of their units in their set-up area (see deployment map). The defending position will have been thoroughly reconnoitred by the attacking force and so there can be no hidden set-up (see Hidden Set-Up in the Konflikt '47 rulebook, page 120).

Once the defender has set up all their units, the attacker deploys their forces in their allocated set-up area. All the attacker's units can be setup with the hidden set-up special rule.

Special Rules

In this scenario the defender's reserves may not use the outflanking manoeuvre special rule and must enter from their own table edge.

Scenario 1: Night Raid

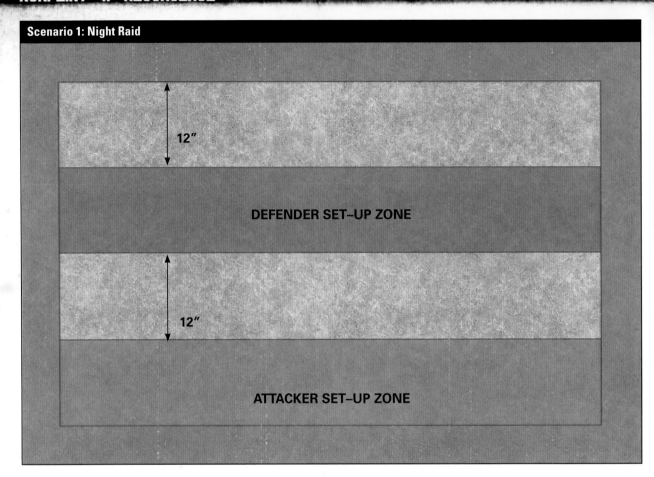

Reduced Visibility

As the raid is being conducted at night this scenario uses the night fighting special rules (see page 85). The scenario is fought using the standard night fighting rules. Both players get the option to declare that they would like to play under the Flare! special rule. If only one player wishes to do so a flare is launched on a roll of 5 or more. If both players wish to use Flare! then flares are launched on a 4 or more as normal.

Objective

The attacker must try to inflict as much damage as possible on the defender whilst conserving their force and escaping from the battle before any counter-attack can be brought to bear. The defender must try to protect their initial force and buy time for the arrival of their reserves. Destruction of the enemy raiding force is a secondary objective.

First Turn

The battle begins. Note there is no first wave in this scenario. All units not held in reserve are deployed at the start of the game.

Game Duration

Keep a count of how many turns have elapsed as the game is played. At the end of Turn 6, roll a die. On a result of 1, 2 or 3 the game ends, on a roll of 4, 5 or 6 play one further turn. The game will also end if there are no longer any attacking force units left on the table at any time.

Victory!

At the end of the game calculate which side has won by adding up victory points as follows:

- The attacker scores 2 victory points for every enemy unit destroyed. They also score 1 victory point for each of their own units, which did not start in reserve that leaves the battle from their own table edge before the end of the game.
- The defender scores 1 victory point for every enemy unit destroyed. They also score 3 victory points for each unit of their initial force (any unit which did not start the game in reserve) which finishes the game in the defender's half of the table.

If one side scores at least 2 more victory points than the other, then that side has won a clear victory. Otherwise the result is deemed too close to call and honours are shared – a draw!

SCENARIO 2: FEINT

In order to draw forces away from the main attack, your unit has been ordered to conduct a feint against an enemy force in your sector. You are to distract the enemy by seeking combat with him. The attack must appear plausible but not be costly!

Forces

This scenario is designed to be played with equal points values on both sides.

Set-Up

Both players roll a die. The highest scorer decides whether to be the attacker or the defender.

If the attacker wishes they may then nominate to roll for a night assault. Roll one die; on a roll of 4+ the reduced visibility rules are in effect for the battle. A further D6 roll is then made on the night fighting table to determine the exact type of night battle to be played (Dawn Assault, Flare!, Longest Day, etc.).

NIGHT FIGHTING TABLE	
1	Dawn Assault
2	Longest Day
3–4	Flare!
5–6	Night

Deployment

The defender picks a side of the table and places up to half their units in their set-up area (see below). These units can use the hidden set-up rules (see Hidden Set-up in the core rulebook, page 120). Units that are not set-up to start with are left in reserve (see Reserves in the core rulebook, page 122).

The attacker's units are not set up on the table at the start of the game. The attacker must nominate at least half of their force to form the first wave. This can be their entire army if they wish. Any units not included in the first wave are left in reserve.

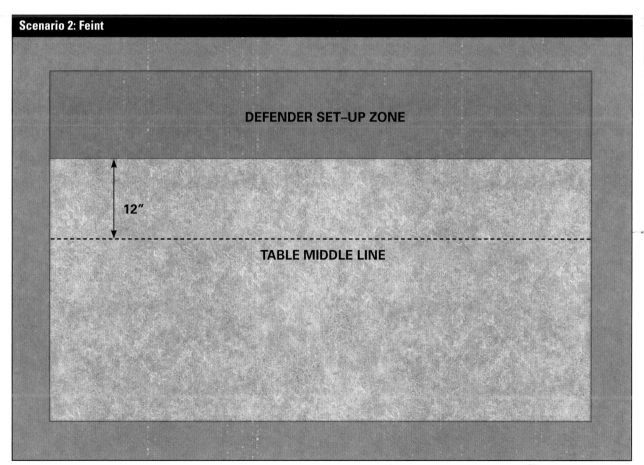

Scenario 2: Feint

DEFENDER SET-UP ZONE

12"

TABLE MIDDLE LINE

US Heavy Infantry ambush Japanese Exoskeleton soldiers

Objective

The attacker must inflict as many casualties on the defender as possible to make the feint appear plausible whilst preserving their force. The defender must hold their position whilst not allowing their reserves to be drawn into the fight and fall for the feint.

First Turn

The battle begins. During Turn 1, the attacker must bring their first wave onto the table. These units can enter the table from any point on the attacker's table edge, and must be given either a Run or Advance order. Note that no order test is required to move units onto the table as part of the first wave.

SNLF Trooper

Game Duration

Keep a count of how many turns have elapsed as the game is played. At the end of Turn 6, roll a die. On a result of 1, 2 or 3 the game ends, on a roll of 4, 5 or 6 play one further turn. If at the end of any turn, the defender has no forces on the table, the game ends.

Victory!

At the end of the game calculate which side has won by adding up victory points as follows:

- The attacker scores 2 points for destroying each defending unit that started on the table destroyed and 2 points for every unit the defender brings on from reserve.
- The defender scores 2 point for every attacking unit destroyed.

If one side scores at least 2 more victory points than the other, then that side has won a clear victory. Otherwise the result is deemed too close to call and honours are shared – a draw!

SCENARIO 3: DELAY

Your force is hard pressed by the enemy and, in order to allow other friendly forces to recover and consolidate, you must trade time for space and slow the enemy's advance.

Forces

This scenario is designed to be played with equal points values on both sides.

Set-Up

Both players roll a die. The highest scorer decides whether to be the attacker or the defender. The defender organises their force into three equal groups; any excess units can be allocated to any group so long as no more than one additional units is added to each group. The defender then nominates either end of the board as the entry edge for the attacking forces.

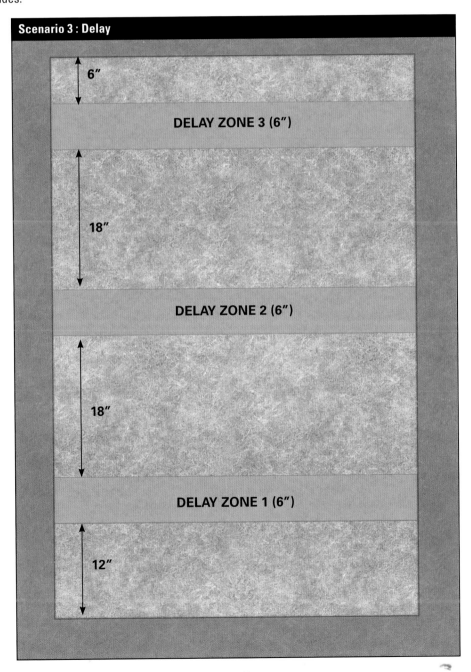

Scenario 3 : Delay

6"

DELAY ZONE 3 (6")

18"

DELAY ZONE 2 (6")

18"

DELAY ZONE 1 (6")

12"

If the attacker wishes they may nominate to roll for a night assault. Roll one die; on a roll of 4+ the reduced visibility rules are in force for the battle. A further roll is then made on the night fighting table to determine the exact type of night battle to be played (Dawn Assault, Flare!, Longest Day, etc.).

NIGHT FIGHTING TABLE	
1	Dawn Assault
2	Longest Day
3–4	Flare!
5–6	Night

Deployment

The defender places each group of units in a separate delay zone as per the deployment map. These units can use the hidden set-up rules (see Hidden Set-up in the Konflikt '47 rulebook, page 120).

The attacker's units are not set up on the table at the start of the game. The attacker must nominate at least half of their force to form the first wave. This can be their entire army if they wish. Any units not included in the first wave are left in reserve (see Reserves in the Konflikt '47 rulebook, page 122).

Preparatory Bombardment

The attacker rolls a die: on a 2+, a preparatory bombardment strikes the enemy positions (see Preparatory Bombardment on page 121 of the Konflikt '47 rulebook). On a result of 1, the barrage fails to materialise, but you have your orders and the attack must go ahead regardless.

Defensive withdrawal

The defender may withdraw units by moving them off his table edge during any turn. Total the starting number of units in the defender's force; the defender can potentially prevent an attacker victory at the end of the game if they have managed to withdraw half (rounding up) of their starting units.

Objective

The attacker must try to progress along the table as quickly as possible. The defender must slow their advance and delay the enemy as long as possible without allowing their force to be decisively engaged (they must live to fight another day!).

First Turn

The battle begins. During Turn 1, the attacker must move their first wave onto the table. These units can enter the table from any point on the attacker's table edge, and must be given either a Run or Advance order. Note that no order test is required to move units onto the table as part of the first wave, and remember that they cannot assault on the turn they enter the table.

Aussies receive a nasty surprise as Gaikokkaku troops burst into a native village

Game Duration

Keep a count of how many turns have elapsed as the game is played. At the end of Turn 10, roll a die. On a result of 1, 2 or 3 the game ends, on a roll of 4, 5 or 6 play one further turn.

Victory!

At the end of the game calculate which side has won as follows. The attacker wins if they have cleared Delay Zones 1 and 2 (i.e., there are no remaining enemy units in these zones) and have at least one unit in Delay Zone 3 by the end of Turn 10.

Under all other conditions the defender wins.

SCENARIO 4: MEETING ENGAGEMENT

'The good general must know friction in order to overcome it whenever possible.'

Carl von Clausewitz, On War

Your forces have met unexpectedly and rapidly deploy to engage each other. Initially, confusion reigns as both sides try to establish themselves but soon orders come in from your Company HQ. As neighbouring units also come into contact with enemy forces, the battle widens and activity in your sector becomes closely linked to the wider battlefield activity.

Forces

This scenario is designed to be played with equal points values on both sides.

Set-Up

Both players roll a die. The highest scorer picks a side of the table and places their base in their set-up zone at least 8" from the table edge. The other player then places a base in their set up zone at least 8" from their table edge, in the same way. Ideally these bases are represented by a model command post

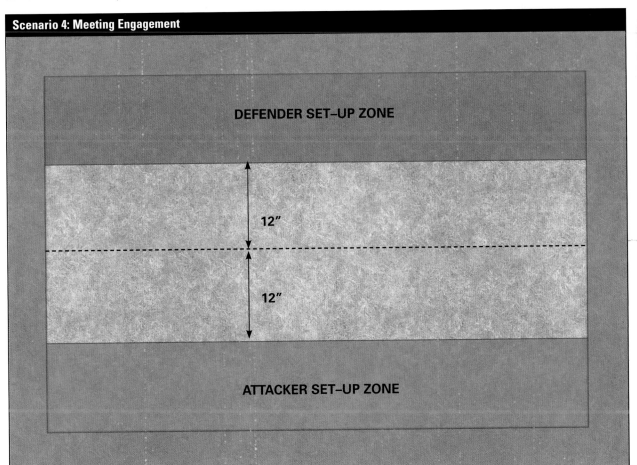

Scenario 4: Meeting Engagement

DEFENDER SET–UP ZONE

12"

12"

ATTACKER SET–UP ZONE

(tent, dug-out, command vehicle), but could be anything that looks like a tactically important position such as a building or hilltop, an ammunition or fuel dump, broken down walker, an artillery or missile battery, etc. A base can simply be a marker or token if you wish– it's entirely up to the players. The important thing is that both players clearly identify their bases at the start of the game. Bases should not be larger than 3" square.

The first player deploys half of the units in their army (rounding down) in their deployment zone.

Units can use the hidden set-up rules (see Hidden Set-up in the Konflikt '47 rulebook, page 120). All other units are left in reserve (see Reserves in the Konflikt '47 rulebook, page 122). Once the first player has deployed as described, their opponent does the same with their own force.

Objective

Initially, forces manoeuvre for control of the battlefield. As orders come in from higher during the battle, forces receive updated objectives throughout the game.

At the beginning of every turn starting from Turn 2, players roll separately on the following table to determine if their objectives change.

Roll	Objective
1	Attack! Orders are received to push the enemy back. You must advance rapidly and penetrate the enemy position.
2–3	Hold! No ground must be ceded to the enemy. You must clear your positions of enemy troops.
4–5	Capture! The ground currently occupied by the enemy has been deemed to be vital to operations. You must capture the position immediately.
6	Withdraw! Command has determined that this is not a battle worth fighting. Commence a withdrawal of your forces.

These objectives are not secret (unless players agree they should be for additional variety). Once a unit has left the battlefield, it may not return.

First Turn

The battle begins. Note there is no first wave in this scenario. All units not held in reserve are deployed at the start of the game.

Game Duration

Keep a count of how many turns have elapsed as the game is played. At the end of Turn 6, roll a die. On a result of 1, 2 or 3 the game ends, on a roll of 4, 5 or 6 play one further turn. If a

Imperial Japanese Army sniper

further turn is taken, repeat this process at the end of Turn 7. The game must end at the end of Turn 8.

Victory!

Throughout the game each player receives 1 victory point for each enemy unit that they destroy. These points are awarded no matter what objective the player is currently working towards.

The objective your force holds on the final turn of the game determines which additional victory points you may claim. You cannot claim for victory points gained whilst you force was under orders for a different objective earlier in the game. Points are awarded as follows:

- Attack! Gain 1 victory point for each unit which has exited off your opponent's board edge.
- Hold! Gain 3 victory points if you hold your own objective.
- Capture! Gain 3 victory points if you hold the enemy's objective.
- Withdraw! Gain 1 victory point for each unit which has exited off your own board edge.

SCENARIO 5: RELIEF-IN-PLACE

Your force has been holding this position for weeks against heavy enemy attack. Your weary troops are due to get relieved today for some much-needed rest. Ever watchful, enemy forces intend to take advantage of the situation and launch a hasty attack to try to wrestle control of the area whilst your forces are vulnerable and trying to extract.

Forces

This scenario is designed to be played with equal points values on both sides.

Set-Up

Both players roll a die. The highest scorer decides whether to be the attacker or the defender.

If the defender wishes they may then nominate to roll for a night battle. Roll one die; on a roll of 6 the reduced visibility rules are in force for the battle. A further roll is then made on the night fighting table to determine the exact type of night battle to be played (Dawn Assault, Flare!, Longest Day, etc.).

Scenario 5: Relief-in-Place

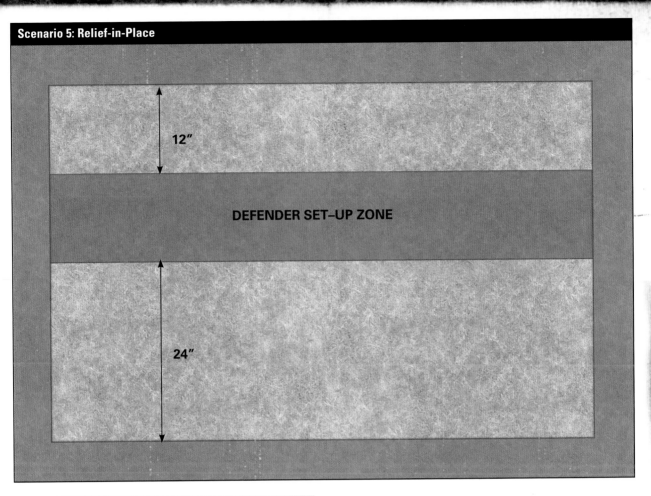

12"

DEFENDER SET–UP ZONE

24"

NIGHT FIGHTING TABLE	
1	Dawn Assault
2	Longest Day
3–4	Flare!
5–6	Night

The defender picks a side of the table and sets up half of their units in their set-up area (see below). These units can use the hidden set-up rules (see Hidden Set-up in the Konflikt '47 rulebook, page 120). Their remaining units form the relieving force. No units may be left in reserve.

As they set up their force, the defender must nominate three separate objectives in their set-up zone. All objectives must be at least 12" from the defender's table edge. In addition, all the objectives must be at least 24" from each other. These objectives could be tactically important positions such as a building or hilltop, or supplies such as an ammo dump or a fuel reserve, or maybe a command post, a walker repair shop, a Rift technology hub or an emplacement for long-range artillery or rocket launchers.

Objectives can be simple markers or tokens if the players prefer, or can be represented by scenic pieces along the lines described above. The important thing is that both players clearly identify the three objectives before the battle begins. The attacker's units are not set up on the table at the start of the game. The attacker must nominate at least half of their force to form their first wave. This can be their entire army if they wish. Any units not included in the first wave are left in reserve (see Reserves in the Konflikt '47 rulebook, page 122).

Objective

The attacker must try and capture the three objectives – the defender must hold these and at the same time, relieve their besieged forces with their relief-in-place force to safely extract their weary initial forces.

First Turn

The battle begins. During Turn 1, the attacker must move their first wave onto the table, and the defender their relieving force. These units can enter the table from any point on the

Scenario 6: Reconnaissance in force

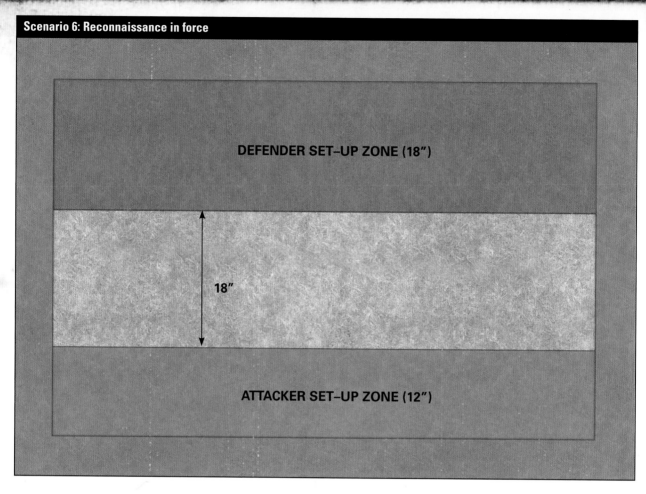

DEFENDER SET–UP ZONE (18")

18"

ATTACKER SET–UP ZONE (12")

player's own table edge, and must be given either a Run or Advance order. Note that no order test is required to move units onto the table during Turn 1.

Game Duration
Keep a count of how many turns have elapsed as the game is played. At the end of turn 6, roll a die. On a result of 1, 2 or 3 game ends, on a roll of 4, 5 or 6 play one further turn.

Victory!
At the end of the game calculate which side has won as follows.

- The attacker scores 2 victory points for each objective they hold and 1 victory point for every defending unit destroyed.
- The defender scores 1 victory point for each objective they hold and an additional victory point for each unit from their initial force that exits the table on their board edge without being destroyed.

All objectives are held by the defender at the start of the game regardless of where their troops are positioned. If an objective changes hands during the game, then it remains under the control of that side until it is taken back.

To capture an objective there must be a model from one of your infantry or artillery units within 3" of the objective at the end of the turn, and there must also be no enemy infantry or field artillery models within 3" of it.

SCENARIO 6: RECONNAISSANCE IN FORCE
Friendly forces are preparing for a large-scale advance, your task is to aggressively find and locate the enemy to feed information back to your higher headquarters for the upcoming battle.

Forces
This scenario is designed to be played with equal points values on both sides.

Set-Up

Both players roll a die. The highest scorer decides whether to be the attacker or the defender. The defender picks a side of the table to hold but does not set up their units until the attacker has placed all their units that are not in reserve. The attacker must deploy at least half their force on the table at the start of the game; all other units are held in reserve (see Reserves in the core rulebook, page 122). Once the attacker's set-up is complete the defender then sets up all of their units in their set-up area. Every one of the defender's units deploys with the hidden set-up rule (see Hidden Set-up in the core rulebook, page 120) and may be dug in; none of the attacker's units may hold either of these conditions. Only the attacker may have units in reserve.

Objective

The attacker must reveal as many hidden units as possible. The defender must prevent the attacker from learning too much about their positions whilst trying to destroy as much of the reconnaissance force as possible.

First Turn

The battle begins. Note there is no first wave in this scenario. All units not held in reserve are deployed at the start of the game

Game Duration

Keep a count of how many turns have elapsed as the game is played. At the end of Turn 5, roll a die. On a result of 1, 2 or 3 the game ends, on a roll of 4, 5 or 6 play one further turn.

Victory!

At the end of the game calculate which side has won by adding up victory points as follows:

- The attacker scores 1 victory point for every defending unit that loses its initial hidden status and 1 victory point for every defending unit destroyed.
- The defender scores 2 victory points for every attacking unit destroyed and 1 victory point for any unit that ends the game hidden.
- If one side scores at least 2 more victory points than the other, then that side has won a clear victory. Otherwise the result is deemed too close to call and honours are shared – a draw!

Japanese Exoskeleton troops push through the undergrowth

CREDITS

Written by
Chris Hale, Ben Moorhouse, and Stu Williams

Artwork by
Jon Cave and Russ Charles

Edited by
Paul Sawyer

Miniatures Designed by
Russ Charles, Duncan Louca, Ben Moorhouse and Warlord Games

Maps, Diagrams and Schematics by
Russ Charles and Ben Moorhouse

Photography by
Aitch Parker, Darek Wyrozebski, Anna Bereza and Mark Owe

Miniatures Painted by
Brush Demon (Ben MacIntyre), Aitch Parker, Ben Moorhouse, Darek Wyrozebski, Andres Amian, Jose Bustamante and Guy Martin

Special Thanks to
John Stallar, Paul Shipman, James Blair, Simon Tams, Stefan Tams, Tatsuya Morikasa, and Louis Moore

US Sherman T